PRAISE FOR *SPURIOUS*

"It's wonderful. I'd recommend the book for its insults alone."
—SAM JORDISON, *THE GUARDIAN*

"Viciously funny."   —*SAN FRANCISCO CHRONICLE*

"I'm still laughing, and it's days later."   —*LOS ANGELES TIMES*

"A tiny marvel ... [A] wonderfully monstrous creation."
—STEVEN POOLE, *THE GUARDIAN*

PRAISE FOR *DOGMA*

"Uproarious."   —*THE NEW YORK TIMES*

"[*Dogma*] brings back W. and Lars, the most unlikely and absurd literary duo since Samuel Beckett's Vladimir and Estragon ... Like *Godot*, this novel is a philosophical rumination, at once serious and playful, on the nature of existence and meaning. While it's comic, there is at bottom a profoundly tragic sense of the chaos and emptiness of modern life. Despair has rarely been so entertaining."
—*LIBRARY JOURNAL*

"Just when my hilarity over the first book of their misadventures, *Spurious*, had faded to a low chuckle, *Dogma* comes along. Between the two books, there's almost no point in breathing, much less coming to any strong conclusions about life, the universe, and everything."   —*LOS ANGELES REVIEW OF BOOKS*

"Witheringly, gut-bustingly funny."   —*THE NEW INQUIRY*

"The epithet 'Beckettian' is perhaps the most overused in criticism, frequently employed as a proxy for less distinguished designations such as 'sparse' or 'a bit depressing.' But Lars Iyer's fiction richly deserves this appellation. His playfully spare—and wryly depressing—landscape, incorporating a bickering double act on a hopeless, existential journey, is steeped in the bathos, farce, wordplay and metaphysics of the man John Calder referred to as 'the last of the great stoics,' its characters accelerating towards a condition of eternal silence, fuelled only by the necessity of speaking out."

—*THE TIMES LITERARY SUPPLEMENT*

PRAISE FOR *EXODUS*

"There is a superfluous joy to these novels ... They are satisfying paradoxes—'difficult' books which are consummately readable; exuberant books about bleakness." —*THE SPECTATOR*

"The saddest, funniest undynamic duo since Vladimir and Estragon ... Like *Spurious* and *Dogma*, *Exodus* is a novel which depends almost entirely on the quality of its scorn. And on any scorn-rating it scores pretty highly." —*THE GUARDIAN*

"Iyer's books aren't so much sad as brimming with good tidings about a utopia that remains pure as long as no one ever does anything ... Like Beckett, they use art to remind us that the whole point is to try, and fail, then try again, and fail better next time." —*HAZLITT*

"The saddest, funniest undynamic duo since Vladimir and Estragon ... Like *Spurious* and *Dogma*, *Exodus* is a novel which depends almost entirely on the quality of its scorn. And on any scorn-rating it scores pretty highly." —*THE GUARDIAN*

"With *Exodus*, as he did with *Spurious* and *Dogma* before it, Iyer has shown that a picaresque novel can be as good a vehicle for philosophy as any." —*RAIN TAXI*

"It was more than a book: it was a revelation, in that Biblical sense of words being exposed down to their meaning, to the *deed in the world* to which they referred." —*THE QUIETUS*

WITTGENSTEIN JR

Also by Lars Iyer

NONFICTION
Blanchot's Communism: Art, Philosophy and the Political
Blanchot's Vigilance: Literature, Phenomenology and the Ethical

FICTION
Spurious
Dogma
Exodus

WITTGENSTEIN JR

LARS IYER

MELVILLE HOUSE
BROOKLYN · LONDON

WITTGENSTEIN JR

Copyright © 2014 by Lars Iyer
First Melville House printing: September 2014

Melville House Publishing   8 Blackstock Mews
145 Plymouth Street   and   Islington
Brooklyn, NY 11201   London N4 2BT

mhpbooks.com   facebook.com/mhpbooks   @melvillehouse

ISBN: 978-1-61219-376-2

Library of Congress Control Number: 2014945089

Design by Christopher King

Printed in the United States of America
1 3 5 7 9 10 8 6 4 2

When you are philosophising you have to descend into primeval chaos and feel at home there.

—Wittgenstein

WITTGENSTEIN JR

1

Wittgenstein's been teaching us for two weeks now.

Was it Ede's idea to call him Wittgenstein? Or Doyle's?

He doesn't *look* like Wittgenstein, it's true. He's tall, whereas the real Wittgenstein was small. He's podgy, whereas the real Wittgenstein was thin. And if he's foreign—European in some sense—he has barely the trace of an accent.

But he has a Wittgensteinian aura, we agree. He is *Wittgensteinisch*, in some way.

He has clearly modelled himself on the real Wittgenstein, Doyle says (and Doyle knows about these things). He dresses like Wittgenstein, for one thing—the jacket, the open-necked shirt, the watch strap protruding from his pocket. And he *behaves* a bit like Wittgenstein too: his intensity—his lips are thinner than any we've seen; his impatience—the way he glared at Scroggins for coming in late; his visible despair.

And of course, like the real Wittgenstein, he has come to Cambridge to do *fundamental work in philosophical logic*.

He sits on a wooden chair at the top of the room, bent forwards, elbows on his knees. His gaze is directed downwards. His eyebrows are raised, and his forehead is furrowed. He has the appearance of a man in *prayer* (Doyle). Of a *constipated* man (Mulberry).

He doesn't *prepare* his teaching. He doesn't *lecture from notes*. At most, he produces a scrap of paper from his pocket and reads out a phrase, or a sentence. He wants simply to *think aloud about certain problems*, he says.

Sometimes he writes a word or two on the blackboard on the mantelshelf. In the first week: *Denken ist schwer* (thought is hard). In the second: *Everything is what it is, and not another thing*. Today: *I will teach you differences*.

None of us understands the problems he is wrestling with, we agree. None of us can follow his *method*—what is he looking for?

Not all of us care, of course. Mulberry is drawing cocks in his notebook. Guthrie wears sunglasses over closed eyes. Benwell groans audibly when Wittgenstein asks him a question.

When will he actually say something? When will he present an *actual argument*?—Mulberry's taking bets.

He proceeds from reflecting on one question to another. From one remark to another. But when will he answer his questions? And what do his remarks *mean*?

A hand in the air.

DOYLE (humbly): I'm having trouble following the argument.

WITTGENSTEIN: That's because I'm not presenting an argument. I am posing questions, that's all.

DOYLE: I don't understand. I can't follow your class.

WITTGENSTEIN: I have no intention of making myself understood.

DOYLE (imploringly): I have no idea what's going on.

WITTGENSTEIN: That is to the good. At this stage, you should have no idea what's going on.

Silence in class.

DOYLE: Perhaps we aren't bright enough to follow you.

WITTGENSTEIN: Intelligence is nothing—you're all *clever*. It is *pride* that is your obstacle. It is pride that is your enemy as students of philosophy. For pride leads you to believe that you are something you are not.

Wittgenstein surveys the room, looking carefully at us. He can see we know ourselves to be *clever*, he says. He can tell we believe ourselves to be full of *Cambridge cleverness*. But that means we're also exposed to the danger of *Cambridge pride*.

We must not think we can hide, he says, scrutinising our faces. The inner life reveals itself in the outer life. It cannot help but do so. The secrets of the inner life are written on the face, he says. They reveal themselves in the simplest gesture. The way you sit on your chair … The way you button or unbutton your jacket …

We must learn to read the face, he says, just as much as we learn to read the page. We must learn to read the *gesture*.

The number of students is falling: forty-five in the first week, twenty-three in the second, eighteen in the third, and this week only twelve. Twelve! An auspicious number, Wittgenstein says. He's glad to be rid of the *hangers-on*.

Twelve faces, to give him the sense that he is not alone. That there are others who might follow the movement of his thinking. He is glad there are others who need to be brought along with him, who might *accompany* him.

We're thinking *with* him: Don't we understand?

Naturally, he is suspicious of *impatience*, he says. But he is wary, also, of *patience*—one mustn't wait too long in one's studies.

Of course, he dislikes the stab-in-the-dark answer, he says. But he also dislikes the *ready* answer—all answers must have something wild about them.

Beware clarity!, he says. Beware the well-trodden path! But beware obscurity, too! Beware the never-trodden path!

Avoid explanation, he says. But also avoid obfuscation. Suspect conclusions. But suspect inconclusiveness, too.

The Backs, along the Cam. The colleges in a row across the river. Ivied walls and trim lawns sloping down to the water. Gloomy clouds, very low.

Twelve students and their teacher—walking to *wash off their brains*. Wittgenstein, hurrying along, his hands behind his back. Okulu, a few paces behind, his hands behind his back. Chakrabarti, a few paces to the left of Okulu, his hands behind his back. Whippet-like Doyle, his hands behind his back. The Kirwin twins, their hands behind their backs. Benwell, scowling, close to the river's edge. Guthrie, singing his hangover song. Mulberry, stripped to his *FUCK YOU* T-shirt, texting on his phone. Ede, sauntering, looking refined. Scroggins, looking spaced out.

Wittgenstein says nothing. The rest of us report on our summer. Titmuss did India, learning the *Om Namah Shivaya* chant and smoking bhang sadhu-style in the Himalayas. The Kirwins did the Iron Man in Mooloolaba and Lanzarote, and rowed on the Thames. Mulberry did strangers in the dark rooms of Madrid, and ran with the bulls in Pamplona. Doyle did the Edinburgh Fringe, Guthrie in tow, performing their show, *Li'l Leibniz*.

Wittgenstein gestures to the university buildings across the river. None of this is real, he says. None of it.

Then, after a long pause: The world is emptying out. The sky is emptying out …

Silence. We look at one another, confused.

He's trying *see* Cambridge, Wittgenstein says. He's done nothing else since he arrived. But all he sees is rubble.

The famous Wren Library!, he says, and laughs. The famous Magdalene Bridge! Rubble, he says, all rubble!

We look around us—immense courts, magnificent lawns, immemorial trees, towers, buttresses and castellated walls, heavy wooden gates barred with iron, tradition incarnate, continuity in stone, the greatest university in the world: *all rubble?* What does Wittgenstein see that we do not?

Wittgenstein is fervent today. He seems to blaze before us.

Written on the board in capital letters, and underlined three times: LOGIC.

We all know what logic is, he says. It is the study of the laws of thought. Of all the forms of reasoning and thinking. The trouble is, we do not know what logic *means*, he says. What reason *means*.

WITTGENSTEIN: If the laws of logic are not followed correctly, then reason is impossible. If reason is impossible, then what is said has no validity. If what is said has no validity, then what ought to be done remains undone. If what ought to be done remains undone, morals and art are corrupted. If morals and art are corrupted, justice goes astray. If justice goes astray, chaos and evil run amuck.

We're drowsy, some of us hungover. Audible sighs. Guthrie, snoring. Mulberry, wearing a *FUCK ME* T-shirt. Benwell, gouging out an obscenity in his desk with a compass point. The Kirwin twins, Alexander and Benedict, in sweatbands and shorts, fresh from rowing. Doyle, in velvet, looking theatrical. Ede, in a sports jacket, refinedly attentive. Titmuss, with his dreads and his pointless wispy beard. Chakrabarti, with his Cambridge University sweatshirt. Scroggins, half high as usual, mouth agape. Okulu, listening to Brahms on his oversize headphones.

A whiteboard full of logical symbols. Who does he think we are, that we could follow him? Who does he take us to be?

Wittgenstein fixes his eyes on the parquet floor.

He tells us about the *vistas* of logic. About logic's *austerity*.

Logic makes you *lose* the world, he says. Logic drives you away from the world, into the eternal ice and snow.

You could say he's only sat at his desk for a few idle hours, he says. You could say he's only opened and closed a few books. You could say he's risked nothing more than paper cuts.

But there are *dangers* to logic, he says. There's its *difficulty*— the arduous training necessary in philosophy, in mathematics. And there's its *purity*—its reflections on thinking itself. Logic can cut you off from the world, he says. You can lose yourself in logic's hall of mirrors.

He's inclined to think of logic as a *sickness*, he says. As a fever on the brow of thought. As the demented smile of a madman.

Logic is only for those who cannot leave it alone, he says.

He seems upset. His voice trembles.

What nonsense he has said, he murmurs. What nonsense we have *made him* say.

Eating in class. Mulberry, chewing gum. Titmuss, sucking mints. Doyle, eating a packet of crisps and regretting it: the crackling! the rustling! the grease! Doyle, closing the packet when Wittgenstein glares at him.

Drinking in class. Guthrie's water bottle, full of gin. Mulberry's juice carton, squeaking as he sucks. Titmuss's energy drink, fizzing over when he pulls it open. Titmuss, blushing bright red, wiping up the mess with his sweater sleeve as Wittgenstein stares at him in disgust.

Toilet breaks. Who dares ask permission to go? Who dares interrupt him? Who dares break into his tense, tortured silences? Scroggins, one afternoon, all but *ran* out of class, knocking over an empty seat as he passed. Wittgenstein looked up, mid-sentence, but said nothing. Titmuss left three times during one session, pleading *Delhi belly*.

WITTGENSTEIN: Haven't you got any *self-discipline*?

The view from the classroom window. Trees losing their leaves. The football pitch, with its churned-up grass, and its thick white lines, newly applied, and its goalposts, newly painted. It looks cold outside. But we are inside, taking notes, understanding almost nothing.

Down by the river, watching the Kirwins in their wetsuits waiting for rowing practice.

They're so tall! You get so much Kirwin for your money! And there's two of them, of course. There'll always be a spare Kirwin.

They're like great prize bulls, we agree. Like a pair of twenty-two-hand Shire horses. The Kirwins must be *for* something. They must have some purpose. It's impossible to imagine the Kirwins without a *Destiny*. They're like Greek heroes. Like something out of Homer.

Mulberry speaks of his desire to fuck a Kirwin. To *lick* a Kirwin. What are the chances of that?

EDE: What about Wittgenstein? Would you like to lick him, Mulberry?

MULBERRY: Not my type. He's gay, though. I can tell. He's a *virgin* gay. A bit like you, Peters.

ME: I'm not a virgin gay!

MULBERRY: You have a thing for Wittgenstein, anyone can see that. You want to be fucked by genius. Well, perhaps you'll have your chance.

EDE: The real Wittgenstein was gay, of course.

MULBERRY: He was another of them: a virgin gay. He never fucked anyone.

EDE: I thought he had boyfriends.

MULBERRY: Oh, he had boyfriends, but they didn't have sex. It wasn't physical.

EDE: Then they weren't boyfriends. They were just romantically coloured friendships.

MULBERRY: Just like you and Peters.

EDE: I, as it happens, am as straight as a die. As for Peters, I cannot say.

A Wittgenstein sighting.

The high street on a warm Saturday. Walking home with our groceries. Then, there he is: Wittgenstein, with his groceries. Wittgenstein with his shopping bags, walking towards us through the other shoppers.

Will he acknowledge us? Will he nod his head? Does he even know who we are?

He nods, murmurs a greeting, passes by.

We walk home in the sun.

EDE: So, genius shops at *Sainsbury's*. Did you see what was in his bags?

ME: Scones, so far as I could see.

EDE: So, genius eats scones.

ME: I think the scones are for us, for our visits.

Wittgenstein has said we are to visit him in his rooms, one by one.

Late night in the *Maypole*, sitting outside in the cold.

Where does Wittgenstein come from?, we wonder. He sounds German, but his English is perfect.

EDE: Perhaps he was educated over here. We had Germans at my school. Actually, we had all kinds of people. Oligarchs' offspring, dictators' sons, sent to acquire some *English polish* ...

MULBERRY: Do they still *beat* pupils at Eton? Are there still *fags*?

EDE: Oh, that's long gone. It's all counselling and bullying workshops now.

It was the same at his school, Mulberry says. He would have liked being beaten.

SCROGGINS: What's it like being *really posh*, Ede? Do you have manservants?

Mulberry says he wishes *he* had a manservant.

DOYLE: Do you call your father *Pater*, Ede?

SCROGGINS: Have you met the Queen, Ede?

TITMUSS: What about Prince Charles?

DOYLE: Aren't you sixth in line for the throne, or something?

Ede is from one of the really ancient families, he says. There's a long line of Edes stretching back before the Conqueror—a whole *dynasty*, with painted portraits hung up and down their stairs, and coats of arms emblazoned over their chimneypieces.

Edes played at being knights at court, serving the monarch in council and government, Ede says. Edes starred in court masques, and kept their heads down after the execution of the king. Come the Restoration, Edes commissioned new country houses, celebrating the *beauty of order*, with Doric colonnades and winged griffins and tripod urns. Edes waved at the natives from the backs of caparisoned elephants in the colonies.

And when the new century came, modern Edes died in blood and fire alongside common folk in the trenches, and married the daughters of the new tycoons of America and South Africa to finance their country estates. Edes kept up the old ways, selling off chunks of their land, hiring out their old halls as wedding venues, and heading to the House of Lords once a week to exercise their ancient privileges.

There were failures in Ede's family, to be sure. Insane Edes, driven mad from inbreeding, hidden in attics ... Failed-suicide Edes, wheeled around in darkened houses ... But in every generation, an Ede steps up. Cometh the hour, cometh the Ede who will pull it all together: the Ede who will become a man of the City, with a pied-à-terre in Richmond, and who will keep the family investments going; the Ede who will see to it that the family fortune grows and grows, and the country estate continues to stand; the Ede who will visit the old pile on the weekends, pulling on his Wellingtons and striding about the ancient grounds ...

DOYLE: And you're that Ede, I suppose?

EDE: I am that Ede.

Half of the class have paid their visits to Wittgenstein's rooms. A pattern has emerged. He directs questions at you, and you reply, as best as you can. He asks about your parents, about your siblings. About the place you grew up.

Scroggins reports on the *austerity* of Wittgenstein's rooms. Their white walls. The two wooden chairs, one for the host, one for the guest, and the card table between them, for the tea tray. He thinks he did poorly, he says. He's not sure why.

Alexander Kirwin describes the buttered scones that Wittgenstein served on a dish; Benedict Kirwin, the metal teapot and two enamel cups, brought in on a tray.

Wittgenstein likes his tea very *weak*, Mulberry testifies; he poured a cup for himself almost as soon as he filled the teapot. And he brought a pan and brush from the kitchen to sweep the crumbs from the table.

Titmuss talked India, he says. His gap year. Wittgenstein seemed interested (EDE: Believe me, Wittgenstein wasn't interested). Okulu took note of the bookshelves—Augustine in Latin. Freud's book on dreams. Marcus's *Meditations*. Unknown volumes in Cyrillic. In ancient Greek.

Memorable things Wittgenstein said. To Scroggins: *It is never difficult to think. It is either easy or impossible.* To Okulu: *What stands between us and good philosophy is the will, not the intellect.* And then, *We must refine the will.* To Titmuss: *You must know who you are, in order to think without deceit.* To Chakrabarti, he said that he was looking for a just word. For a *new language of creation.* To Doyle: *We are latecomers. Disinherited children.* And then: *We are without tradition. Without belief.*

The *unity* of his teaching. That's what he wants us to perceive, he says. His teaching depends on its *cumulative* effect.

The recurrence of certain topics, and the disappearance of others. Are we beginning to sense a pattern?

The *rhythm* of his lecturing. The long pauses he leaves between remarks: is it intended as a kind of punctuation? Of *syncopation?*

Sometimes he pauses in his teaching to pose questions, and reacts to our replies.

When one of us says something helpful, he raises his eyebrows, and says, *Go on.* But when he hears something he finds *un*helpful, his eyebrows fall again.

Helpful: Ede's remark about indiscernibles. Doyle's remark about syllogistic form.

Unhelpful: Okulu's remark about deduction. Alexander Kirwin's reply about *in*duction.

Altogether irrelevant: Chakrabarti's remark about *sub*duction. Scroggins's remark about *pro*duction.

Entirely facetious: Benwell's sotto voce remark about alien *ab*duction.

Competition in class: Who can hold their breath the longest? Guthrie tries, holding his breath for a few minutes, before gasping loudly. Mulberry tries, and collapses, blue-faced, on the floor.

WITTGENSTEIN (vexed): What's the matter with you, man?

Notes passed in class. Mulberry to Doyle: *You're a whiny little bitch.* Doyle to Mulberry: *You have a micro-penis.* Mulberry to Doyle: *You have a nano-penis.* Doyle to Mulberry: *You have a quantum penis. It's both there and not there.*

Fights in class. Mulberry punches Doyle, giving him a dead arm. Doyle *pinches* Mulberry, making him squeal out loud.

Wittgenstein, quoting: *Anything a man knows, anything he has not merely heard rumbling and roaring, can be said in three words. He* hears only rumbling and roaring, he says. *Our* rumbling and roaring.

The view from the window. Heavy gulls, though we're far from the sea. The wind tearing the last leaves from the tree. The groundskeeper, with a roller, flattening the turf.

How cold it is out there! And how *dark* it's getting, even though it's only mid-afternoon!

One more year of study before we have to go outside. Actually, it's only four-fifths of a year now, before the wind will whip around us ...

Will we really have to go out there? Will we have to make our way in the world? Not now. Not yet. We're not ready ...

Standing in the corridor, waiting for the previous class to finish. It's five minutes past the hour.

Wittgenstein, staring at the door, leather satchel under his arm. Wittgenstein, rocking on his toes. Wittgenstein, knocking loudly. Opening the door ...

WITTGENSTEIN (severely): Excuse me, would you mind ...

Students file out, and then the lecturer, to whom Wittgenstein bows slightly.

A PowerPoint presentation on the whiteboard. Bullet points. Pictures. Leftover handouts on the desks. Photocopied excerpts from an introductory book.

Where is *our* list of *key concepts*? Where are *our aims and objectives*? Where are the learning outcomes for *our* lectures? Where is *our virtual learning environment*?

His classes are just a series of remarks, separated by silences. Ideas, in haiku-like sentences, full of delicate beauty and concision.

Each remark concentrates in itself all of his teaching, he says. Each remark crouches like a wolf ready to pounce, for the one who can hear what he is saying.

DOYLE: How are we meant to know what lies behind your remarks?

WITTGENSTEIN (the quote marks audible): Nothing lies 'behind' my remarks.

DOYLE: Is there some theory you're trying to express?

WITTGENSTEIN: I am trying to think, that's all. I am trying to ask questions.

DOYLE: Then what are we supposed to learn from your lectures?

WITTGENSTEIN: Structures. That's all I want you to see. *Depths.*

DOYLE: But I can't see anything!

Wittgenstein turns over the most ordinary words for inspection. He insists on beginning anew. On starting again, all over again. On discarding *false* beginnings. On struggling to a yet more originary beginning, on pushing back to ever deeper fundaments. On swimming against the current, against all satisfaction.

There are moments of apparent progress in his class. Moments of clarification, when he smiles bleakly. But then, there is the perpetual return of doubt. Of despair. Of *failure*.

He leans forward in his chair, eyes closed. Then, opening his eyes, he looks up at us, with a pained expression on his face.

There is something he hasn't yet *realised*, he says. Something he hasn't *seen*. If only it could be *shown* to him.

His torment. Halfway through class, he utters a loud cry. He's giving up logic for good, he says. He'd have made a better *clown* than logician.

A long pause, before he starts again.

If a man could write a book on philosophy, which was really a book on philosophy, this book would, with an explosion, destroy all the other books in the world, he quotes.

He is trying to write such a book, he says. The *Logik. Die Logik.*

Wittgenstein, on his chair at the front of the room. Who will come with him to wash off his brain?

Outside. Wittgenstein, walking ahead of us. Students in surging groups. Students everywhere, a sea of them, moving in fast currents.

Posh students everywhere. Rah boys in gilets and flip-flops, with piles of bed-head hair. Rugby types, as big as fridges, all red-cheeked health, their voices booming. Rah girls dressed down in gym gear and pony-tails. English roses in horse-and-hound clothing, as though fresh from the gymkhana. Yummy not-yet-mummies in fur-lined Barbour. Ethno-Sloanes, with string tops and slouch-bags. Sloane-ingénues with big cups of coffee, sweater sleeves half pulled over their hands ...

EDE: The *Cambridge type*. Revolting! When was the last time you met anyone *working class* at Cambridge?

DOYLE: There's Benwell.

EDE: He's hardly typical. Besides, he wants nothing to do with us.

We consider the enigma of Benwell. Why does he always scowl at us, though we, too, attend Wittgenstein's class? Why does he ignore us?

Ede thinks it must be a northern thing. Things are grim up there.

DOYLE: Peters is northern!

EDE: Well, Benwell is from farther north. The real north.

Ede conjures up an image of Benwell in his old pit village, wandering past slag heaps and barred factory gates. Past rasping ex-miners on mobility scooters, past workless lads and grey-faced mothers, past the drug-addled and the muttering mad, up to the lonely moorland ...

Ede says he's always wanted to come from the north. It would legitimate his sense of despair.

MULBERRY: Despair about what? You're as rich as Croesus!

EDE: About everything! If I were Benwell I'd want to blow all this up—the river, the Backs, all of Cambridge ... Actually, if I were Benwell, I'd like to blow *us* up.

Luckily, there are drugs to dull the pain, Ede says, popping a mogadon and taking an extra one for luck.

EDE: This is how I got through Eton.

Wittgenstein, ahead of us, hands behind his back.

DOYLE: What do you suppose he's thinking about?

EDE: Something very, very difficult.

DOYLE: Why does philosophy have to be so *hard*?

EDE: You don't know you're doing philosophy unless it *hurts*. Feel the burn, Doyle-o!

Wittgenstein points out the faded names of firms on the sides of buildings. Names carved from building stone. Buildings once had a *purpose*, he says. People, too. There was a time when the butcher, the baker and the candlestick maker *really were* the butcher, the baker and the candlestick maker. When the Cambridge don *really was* a don, he says. And when the Cambridge student—any student—*really was* a student.

Trinity Street. The gatehouses, with their turrets ... The filigree of the pinnacles, spires and domes ... The stained-glass windows of King's College Chapel ...

EDE: They put the cobbles in to impress the tourists, you know. Ye olde Cambridge and all that. It's like a stage set. The spectacle of the upper class in their natural setting.

WITTGENSTEIN (turning to face us): The beauty of Cambridge is meant to *lull* you, to make you let down your defences. The eye is only *distracted* by beauty. It is only *deceived* by beauty. Because the old alliance between beauty and goodness has long been broken, and the treaty between beauty and truth was torn up some time ago.

EDE (quietly): That was *my* point.

King's Parade. Teenage tourists pose against the college walls. One pretends to hold the gatehouse of St John's between his fingers, another does handstands. A clump of child-tourists are ushered away from the grass by a security guard.

Only the tourists really understand Cambridge, Wittgenstein says. Cambridge is *only there to be photographed*: that's what they grasp. Cambridge is a collective *fantasy* ...

Ede's rooms.

EDE (doing his Wittgenstein impression): Cambridge dissolving ist. Like ein Alka-Seltzer.

ME (doing my Wittgenstein impression): *Die Logik* mit ein kicking *k*!

Laughter. How absurd Wittgenstein is! How pompous!

Still, it would be really something to make an impression on him, we agree. To say something startling in class, to make him look up, surprised. *Perhaps you have something there*, he'd say. *You have put your finger on something*, he'd say. Or: *You have said something much more important than you realise.* Or: *Yes, that is certainly worth thinking about.* Or: *You have identified a genuine issue.* Or: *I must think about this further.*

Imagine Wittgenstein making reference to you in class. *As Ede said to me the other day* . . . Or: *Peters raised an interesting point with me* . . .

Imagine walking through the cloisters with Wittgenstein, solving some logical problem together, voices echoing. Or standing on the library steps, exchanging ideas with hushed vehemence. Or walking silently in thought alongside him on the Backs, musing on some great Problem . . .

EDE: Wouldn't it be nice to be brilliant? *Philosophically* brilliant! *Logically* brilliant! Wouldn't you like to show *witty* brilliance, at least? A brilliance of repartee at the dinner table? Wouldn't you like to be a *savant*, who people fear for and look after? Or a *drunken* genius, who comes into his own in kebab shops at 4 AM?

We speak of brilliance *stumbling* as night becomes dawn. Of brilliance passed out in a flowerbed. Of brilliance sick on the cobblestones ... Of *stray* brilliance, wandering from every track ...

We speak of burning yourself up from the effort of thinking. Of being *spent* from thinking, like an exhausted horse ... Of your life being merely the *husk* of thought, of the effort to think ...

And for Wittgenstein himself to sit at your bedside, as you expired from thought. For Wittgenstein himself to watch over you, mopping your brow, as you *died* from thought ...

Wednesday evening. Ede tells me about his visit to Wittgenstein.

He knocked at the door, exactly on the hour, and almost instantly felt watched through the grille. Then the door opened, and there was Wittgenstein. He seemed *frail*, despite his height, Ede says. Vulnerable.

Ede felt nervous, he says. A little drunk, though he hadn't drunk a thing. He thought he was going to say something stupid.

Wittgenstein asked his usual questions. Ede let out that he was heir to a duchy—he's not sure why. Wittgenstein nodded. He, too, has known privilege, he said.

Ede needed the loo. He asked him where the toilet was, and felt vulgar.

So Ede stood pissing in Wittgenstein's toilet. He felt he ought to have *sat* on the toilet to piss, he says. He noticed the dried lavender in a little pot in the bathroom. A tube of Aquafresh beside a toothbrush.

EDE: Genius uses Aquafresh.

Ede felt like a dolt through it all, he says. He couldn't express himself. He couldn't say anything witty. Anything memorable. But then, there wasn't much *space* to speak. It's *Wittgenstein's* show, not yours, Ede says. Wittgenstein's the star, even if he pretends he isn't.

But his rooms really are different from other dons', Ede says. There's no wall of leather-bound books. No clutter of collectibles. No kitsch souvenirs as talking points. No bottles of college sherry, one dry and one sweet. No bottles of beer for undergraduates. No *shabbiness*—no sagging armchairs, no coffee-stained rugs. It's very clean, very austere.

EDE: He told me about his hot baths. He boasted about the temperatures he can stand. And he said something about his hatred of carpets. *You can't keep them clean!*

There was a flowering plant on Wittgenstein's windowsill, in a little pot, Ede says. And he heard the sound of a piano being practised, a couple of floors down. And he caught a glimpse of Wittgenstein's neatly made bed, through a half-open door. And he saw the views from Wittgenstein's rooms, which look out over the red-tiled roofs, towards the river.

I tell Ede about *my* visit to Wittgenstein. The same stairs, the grille, the tea, the quiz. Wittgenstein set the tone, and I told him all sorts of silly things. My parents' farm. My scholarship. My hatred of boarding school. My nostalgia for the hills of Yorkshire, as compared to the flatness of Cambridgeshire. My fruitless search for the so-called Gog Magog Hills in the Cambridgeshire countryside. My poetry…

EDE: Your poetry! What a sensitive young man you are, Peters.

ME: He quoted Blake. And Cowper.

EDE: Yes, yes, but did you get anything interesting out of him?

ME: He said he doesn't read philosophy any more. *If a book doesn't make you want to throw it aside and think your own thoughts, what use is it?*, he said. And another thing: he has a brother.

EDE: Really!?

ME: Yes, he mentioned him in passing. *As my brother said of Oxford* ... Something like that.

EDE: *Very* interesting.

Ede opens his laptop and googles *Oxford*, coupled with Wittgenstein's real surname. A news article: *Oxford Don Suicide*.

EDE: *Very, very* interesting—doomed genius. (Then, summarising): The brother was a brilliant young mathematician. A prodigy. Went up to Oxford at fifteen. Finished his doctoral studies at nineteen, when he became a Junior Research Fellow. Took his life at twenty. Well!

How old is Wittgenstein?, we wonder. Twenty-three? Twenty-four? Definitely a potential suicide, we agree.

Ede googles *logic and suicides*, but gets nothing. He googles *maths and madness*.

EDE: Cantor sent himself mad, when he was investigating infinity, apparently. Gödel, too—he starved himself to death ...

The framed picture of Descartes on the classroom wall. (A *degenerate*, Wittgenstein says.) The framed picture of Leibniz. (A *monster of thought*, Wittgenstein says.)

The philosopher *looks* different from other people, Wittgenstein says. The philosopher's face has secrets. Hiding places. The philosopher is incapable of a simple smile.

There are no signs of philosophy in *our* faces, he says, looking round the class. Because we know nothing of *fate*, he says. Nothing of *fatality*. We do not understand what it means to be *destined*.

We are parts of things: that's our luck, he says. The philosopher's misfortune is to be a part of nothing. To stand apart from everything.

To renounce the pomps and vanity of the world, as St Paul said. *I die daily*: just think what that would really mean, Wittgenstein says.

The great risk is that we will lose our souls, Wittgenstein says. There are very few people who do not lose their souls. It will happen to us. Not now, perhaps, but *eventually*. We will be tested. We may gain the whole world, he says—and he's sure many of us will, with our well-off families and our wealth of connections—but this matters little if we lose our souls.

Okulu's organ recital.

Dim light. Medieval glass. The fan-vaulted ceiling.

We're supposed to feel awe, Ede says, looking round the gloom. We're supposed to feel dwarfed.

EDE: The *mysterium tremendum.* Transcendence and all that. The depth of history! Of tradition! Of religion! The mystique of old England, and so on. Well, there is no mystery. We're all out in the open now.

We survey the audience. The Kirwins, in tracksuits. (EDE: You would have thought they'd have made *some* effort!) Scroggins, half asleep. (EDE: He's high as a kite. You can see it.)

A spotlight over the organ.

EDE: Oh God—*culture!* Remind me why we came again?

Okulu, bowing to the audience. Taking his seat.

Rolling waves of Bach in the near-darkness.

The low notes get him right in the *gut*, Ede says. They're loosening his bowels.

The bass notes are giving him an *erection*, Mulberry says.

We notice Wittgenstein below us, hands clasped over his knee. The nape of his neck, smooth and sallow next to the collar of his crisp white shirt.

MULBERRY: Calm yourself, Peters.

ME: Look how *moved* he is. His eyes are closed. What's wrong with us, that we don't feel that way?

EDE: We're English. There's no cure for that.

· · ·

Walking back. Wittgenstein ahead of us.

He never feels anything you're supposed to feel, Ede says. All this art! Music! All these *experiences*!

I tell him I was moved. Very moved.

EDE: It's because you want to be overawed, Peters. That's what culture is for: overawing people like you.

Scroggins and the Kirwins catch up with us.

EDE (quietly): Oh God!

Discussion. Our plans for the Christmas break. A family safari in the heart of Zambia (the Kirwins). Swimming with sharks off the coast of Mauritius (Scroggins). Skiing in the Rockies (Ede—but he's sick of skiing, he says) ...

KIRWIN A: Where are *you* going, Peters? Yorkshire?

KIRWIN B: How's the skiing in Yorkshire, Peters?

KIRWIN A: You're really a bit of a *peasant*, aren't you, Peters?

EDE: Just because Peters isn't an aristo!

KIRWIN B: Well, *we're* not aristos, *technically* speaking. You have to be in Burke's book of peerages to be an aristo.

KIRWIN A: Yes, but we're hardly *scholarship boys*, are we? We haven't known poverty.

KIRWIN B: Alexander thinks that not going skiing constitutes *poverty*.

Ede asks the Kirwins about performance-enhancing drugs. Do they ever take them?

Vehement denials.

EDE: Oh, of course you do. All athletes do. They're supposed to shrink your cocks, performance-enhancing drugs, aren't they? Cock-shrinkage: has that happened to you? Come on, you can tell us.

The Kirwins storm off.

Laughter.

He was just *asking*, Ede says.

ME (looking ahead): What *is* Wittgenstein thinking about?

EDE: Death, I should imagine. Our shortcomings. His own shortcomings. His sense of sin.

We run to catch up with him.

Indian summer.

Ede and I, walking in the open fields by Grange Road.

If only we had something to talk about, like the scholars of yore! Something serious. Something weighty, on which to take sides! We would walk and talk, and talk and walk. We would outline our positions, and refine our ideas …

We would speak of topic *A*, as we walk, stroking our chins, and topic *B*, shaking our heads. We would ponder issue *C* with great sternness, and toss restless ideas back and forth about issue *D*. Patiently, carefully, we would consider the likely repercussions of thesis *E*, and ask whether the consequences of issue *F* have really been thought through. Is hypothesis *G* worthy of consideration?, we'd wonder. And what about conjecture *H*? We would shake our heads about nostrum *I*, and laugh about the preposterousness of fallacy *J*—how could anyone take *J* seriously! *K* is a *heresy*, we would agree, pursing our lips. As for *L*—there's something to be said about *L*, we would agree, nodding our heads …

What is it we lack as intellectuals?, we wonder. Ideas? Real intelligence? Is it a question of temperament? Of *intensity*? Is it a matter of being *European—old* European—or at least *foreign*?

You can't teach love—that's what Wittgenstein said yesterday. That's the *condition* of philosophy: fierce and fiery love. Philosophy is the love of wisdom, he said. A love for what you do not possess. A love for what, nevertheless, has left its trace in you.

Wittgenstein is a lover—that's what we learnt yesterday. A lover's heart beats beneath that dour exterior ...

Do *we* have love—real love—for philosophy?, Ede and I wonder. Are we capable of that love?

We have the sense of living for something larger than us, *better* than us. The sense of something *worthwhile*, that we can serve. We have the sense of something *difficult*, to which we can dedicate ourselves. The sense of being *part* of something, *involved* in something ...

The sky clouding over. The sun slanting in.

We walk, thinking of the many times Wittgenstein has been seen walking in Cambridge, and confiding our desire to *share* in Wittgenstein's walks. To become, if not fellow thinkers, then at least fellow *walkers*, companions in thought.

To walk behind him, wondering about the effect on his thinking of the sun warming his head. Wondering about the effect of heavy rain or thick fog. Wondering about the effect of the crunch of snow underfoot. Wondering if it makes any difference to his thought whether he keeps the river on his left, or on his right. Musing upon the influence of *topography* on his thought. Of elevation, or depression. Pondering the difference between thinking on the valley bottom and on the hillcrest ...

But better still would be to walk *with* him, we agree. To listen to his concerns as we walk together. To walk quietly and listen. To appear to take in his ideas, without understanding a word. To murmur noncommittally as he speaks. To nod our heads mutely, and at the right time. To agree, when we sense he wants agreement, and to disagree, when he seems to want *dis*agreement.

To pause when he takes mind to pause. To stand quietly as

he works out a problem. And to start walking with him as he starts walking again, as his thoughts become unstuck again ...

To take *morning* walks with Wittgenstein! Full of vigour and energy! Full of hope! Full of the promise of the work he will do that day! To take *dawn* walks, the world dew-wet with promise. *Edenic* walks, as Adam took with Eve just after the Creation. Walks in which he would feel his philosophical powers gathering ... Walks in which he would draw the air to the bottom of his lungs ... Walks in which he would nod his head to other early-risers, other kings and queens of the morning ...

To take *afternoon* walks with Wittgenstein! Long and languorous walks. *Wandering* walks, walks without plan, on which he would muse upon the most intractable issues. Walks with the indefinite as their horizon. Walks as wide as the world, as open ...

To take *nighttime* walks with Wittgenstein! After hours, when anything can be said. Walks of confidences, when he might talk hush-voiced of his dreams and desires. When he might whisper to us of secret hopes and fervours. Of his thought-ambitions. Of his *Logik*.

To take walks *after midnight* with Wittgenstein! Walks of the early hours. To take the insomniac's walk, the *too-awake* walk. To take the *over-conscious* walk that would tire him out. How would we help him to find his way to sleep, walking among the last of the revellers and the puddles of vomit?

Wittgenstein, turning to us in desperation. In *vulnerability*. Wittgenstein saying: *Help me! Help me to think!*

Sounds of machine-gun fire. Booms. Shouting. The lecturer in the next room must be showing a film.

Wittgenstein winces.

His silence, our silence. His, a silence of inner struggle. Of armies of thought clashing inside him. Of Jacob wrestling the angel. Ours, a silence of expectancy, giving way to distraction.

A fly on the windowpane. Isn't it too cold for flies ...?

The playing fields, touched with frost. Football noises come through the fog.

A thought must arrive all at once, or not at all, he says.

Spontaneity: that is his aim. To think *spontaneously*, as by a kind of reflex.

We must retrain our *thought-instincts*, he says. We must rehone our most basic *thought-responses*.

Classroom décor. Faded posters. Old bound editions of learned journals in locked cabinets, roman numerals on the spines. Who reads them? What have they to do with anyone? How long have they been here? Did people *ever* read them? Did anyone *ever* care about such things?

The journals make us uneasy. They are not *of* us, not accessible to us. They're not *for* us, yet they surround us. Isn't Cambridge supposed to be *our* playground? Isn't Cambridge supposed to centre on *us*?

Cambridge should be about us—here—in the present. Cambridge should come to *us*, who live in the present ...

The fire alarm. We remain at our desks. Is it a drill? Will it stop? Will silence return? The alarm is persistent. A fire warden bangs on the door. We have to vacate the building.

Outside. Low, dark cloud. We stand about in the drizzle, among all the other students. Mulberry, with his *FUCK TOMORROW* T-shirt. Titmuss, with his new nose ring.

We look at our feet, Wittgenstein looks at the sky. Minutes pass. Everyone around us starts to file back inside.

He can't go in again, Wittgenstein says. We'll have to walk, all of us. We'll have to revive the *peripatetic school*.

The Great Bridge. Magdalene College. The River Cam, muddy and narrow.

How sick he is of Cambridge!, he says. How tired he is!

This foul, damp city, he says. This rotten place. This marsh stagnancy, full of fogs and vapours. This place of *lowness*. This place of *contagion*. He's suffocating, he says.

Imagine it!, he says: a whole town built below sea level (more or less). Waiting for the sea to close over it. Waiting to drown, with just the spires of King's College Chapel poking up above the water.

We walk quietly beside him, wary of his mood.

A don, walking his dog, greets Wittgenstein. Wittgenstein nods back.

The dog is a disgusting creature, Wittgenstein says when the don is out of earshot. Bred for dependency. Bred for slobbering. We think our dogs love us because we have a debased idea of love, he says. We think our dogs are loyal to us because we have a corrupted sense of loyalty.

People object to pit bulls and Rottweilers, but pit bulls and Rottweilers are his *favourite* dogs, Wittgenstein says. They don't hide what they are.

People love Labradors, of course. But the Labrador is the most disgusting of dogs, he says, *because* of its apparent gentleness.

The *kindness* of the Labrador: disgusting. The *pleasantness* of the Labrador: disgusting. The *even-temperedness* of the Labrador: disgusting. The *tractability* of the Labrador: disgusting. The *easygoingness* of the Labrador: likewise disgusting. The *affability* of the Labrador: *altogether* disgusting. The *good-naturedness* of the Labrador: filth! Pure filth! The *outgoingness* of the Labrador: horrific. The *sociability* of the Labrador: despicable. The *kindly eyes* of the Labrador: wholly disgusting ...

The Cambridge dons' thoughts are like their dogs, he says. Their thoughts are like thoughts on a leash ... Thoughts trained to play catch ... Thoughts sniffing the rear ends of other thoughts ... Thoughts with a collar round their necks. Thoughts whose mess you have to clean up.

The Cambridge mistake is to believe that thought simply comes when you whistle, he says. But thought must whistle to us! Thought should not be *tame*! Thought should *tear out our throats*!

Wittgenstein speaks of *dangerous* thoughts, of thoughts which bite. He speaks of *wild* thoughts which snarl and sting. Of thoughts which have to be tamed and broken.

There are thoughts you have to *avoid* if they appear, he says. *Shy* thoughts, *wary* thoughts, thoughts that only cross your mind when all is calm and still, like deer passing through a woodland glade at dawn.

And there are thoughts that have to be *flushed out*, he says. Driven in herds. Thoughts that need *baiting*—thoughts that can be caught only by means of decoys, of lures, of hidden traps. Thoughts for which you have to lie in wait.

And there are thoughts you have to *run down*, he says— thoughts you have to chase through days and nights. Thoughts which run *you* down. Thoughts which turn *you* into the quarry, thoughts which charge *you*, thoughts which beat *you* from *your* hiding place.

And there are thoughts which are cleverer than you are, he says. Wiser than you are. Thoughts which are *better* than you are, loftier and more noble. *High* thoughts, thoughts that stream above you …

And there are thoughts of the *stratosphere*, he says. Of the *ionosphere*! Thoughts that skim along the edge of space, and that you have to bring down to earth. Thoughts of the *depths*— *subterranean* thoughts, which sing through fundaments and profundities. *Reverberant* thoughts, like buried earthquakes. Thoughts no longer of the hard crust, but of the blazing mantle. Thoughts of the earth's core, deep down where lava turns in lava.

Those are the kinds of thoughts he came to Cambridge to think, Wittgenstein says. Those are the thoughts only the *atrocious conditions of Cambridge* might impel him to think.

He didn't come to Cambridge to sit at the feet of Collison-Bell, the modal logician, he says. Nor of Hawley, the modal realist. It wasn't the epistemological work of Pritchett that drew him here, nor the meta-epistemology of McPherson. He didn't come to study with Oliphant, the famous metaphysician, nor to pursue the meta-philosophy of 'Mutt' McDonald. It was not to attend the lectures of Price-Young on *Infallibalism*, nor of Safranski on *Indefeasibility*, nor of Subramanian on *Externalism*, nor of Han on *Internalism*. It wasn't to ally himself with the research group on *Quantum Cognition*, nor to become part of the *Computational Neuroscience Network*. He had no intention whatsoever of advancing Cambridgean thought in the areas of *malleable intelligence*, nor of *dynacism*.

He came to Cambridge to be *close to the thieves*, he says. *Blessed are those who know at what time of night the thieves will come. They will be awake, gathering their strength and strapping on their belts, before the thieves arrive.*

It is night, he says. He is strapping on his belt. Because he came to Cambridge to *rout the thieves*.

(EDE (whispering): Isn't Wittgenstein, technically, a don?

ME (whispering): But not *spiritually*. And that's the point.)

Little St Mary's Church, damp and quiet. Bottled-up air. The smell of wet plaster.

It's really only the fragment of a church, you can see that, Wittgenstein says. It was meant to be part of something larger.

He admires the flintwork of the tower. Cambridgeshire flint, he says, the only stone round here. He admires the windows, and the daggers and mouchettes in the tracery. So similar to Ely Cathedral, he says. So unlike other East Anglian churches …

A long pause. The rest of us stand about awkwardly. Wittgenstein smiles. The problem is, none of us really knows what to *do* in a church, he says.

We know we have to be quiet, he says. We know we mustn't *disturb* the church. Even Benwell knows that he shouldn't make a racket in the calm. But that's all that remains of the old reverence for the place where heaven and earth were supposed to meet.

WITTGENSTEIN (inspecting the chantry chapels): Christianity declares us to be wretched: that's its greatness. Christianity knows us as sinners. (A pause.) I suppose you are all atheists.

Titmuss begins to speak of religion in India. No one listens.

MULBERRY: Do *you* believe in God?

WITTGENSTEIN: I do not. Not, at least, in the sense you think I might.

MULBERRY: Surely you either believe in God or you don't.

WITTGENSTEIN: Perhaps it is not a question of belief. Perhaps the concept of God is not the kind of thing in which one can believe or disbelieve.

DOYLE: You mean religion is a *cultural* thing? That it's all about belonging to a tradition?

Silence.

WITTGENSTEIN: A despairing man cries, *O God*, and rolls his eyes up to heaven. It is on that basis we should understand both the words *God* and *heaven*. A despairing man cries, *I am damned*, and falls, weeping, to the ground. It is on that basis we should understand both the words *damnation* and *Hell*.

The concept of God is used to express an *extremity of wretchedness, suffering, and doubt*, he says. Really, religion is only for the wretched. That's why we, who know nothing of wretchedness, know nothing of religion. And that's why we, who never feel ourselves to be wretched, know nothing of philosophy, either.

A painting of St Michael, weighing souls in his scales. Of St Christopher, crossing a great river with the infant Christ on his shoulder.

Titmuss's phone goes off (who else would have a *Govinda Jaya Jaya* ringtone?). He fumbles through his pockets.

Come, let's go, Wittgenstein says. We shouldn't wake the church. The church is dreaming. The church is falling through the centuries. The church doesn't want to be woken up. It doesn't want us here.

Trumpington Street. A sudden shower. Rain, falling heavily. We shelter in the museum porch, watching the water splash from the gutters.

TITMUSS: It's like an Indian monsoon. The weather's gone weird.

EDE: The world's ending.

MULBERRY: And Cambridge will be the first to go under. Cambridge and Cambridgeshire and East Anglia ... The North Sea will reclaim it all.

EDE: You seem pleased.

MULBERRY: Oh, I can't *wait* for the world to end!

Rain pours from the mouths of the gargoyles. Chained monkeys ... A drowning monk ... A faceless figure with a snake in its mouth ...

WITTGENSTEIN: Do you know why God sent the Flood? Men spilled their seed on trees and stones. They copulated with beasts. And the greater beasts copulated with lesser beasts—the dog, with the rat; the cock, with the peahen. (A pause.) So God *reversed* the act of creation, unleashing the sea he had once sealed up, allowing the waters of the deep to sweep over the land.

TITMUSS (quietly): Far out, man.

MULBERRY (quieter still): You're a fucking hippie, Titmuss.

•   •   •

Inside the Fitzwilliam, sheltering from the rain.

His brother thought of himself as a kind of *Noah*, Wittgenstein says, as we wander among the exhibits.

Logic is what guards against the Flood, his brother said. Against the annulment of order. Against the destruction of goodness.

Noah sought a sanctuary on the face of the abyss, his brother wrote in his notebooks. *And isn't that what I am seeking: a sanctuary on the face of the abyss?*

As love is stronger than death, so is logic stronger than chaos, his brother wrote in his notebooks. *In the storm of the world, the ark of my thought will anchor on the mountain of certainty.*

Guy Fawkes'. Midnight, after the pubs close. Mulberry's annual *derangement of the senses* house party.

Coats in the front room. DJ in the living room. Dealer in the dining room, showing his wares: MDMA, 'Miaow Miaow', and a mystery powder he can't identify. An *amuse-bouche*, he says—a free snort for anyone who buys …

The kitchen. Dozens of cans of beer, wine. A jam-tub full of punch, with floating cherries and slices of banana. Stacks of plastic cups wrapped in cellophane.

The first bedroom upstairs. Very grand, with sanded floorboards and tall sash windows looking out onto the street. The marijuana zone. Posters: Che in his beret, Bob Marley in Rasta colours. We join the smoking circle.

Conversation is dopey, making Ede impatient. Where are the Clare College girls Mulberry promised? Ede needs girls!

EDE: Have you ever been in love, Peters? I mean *really* in love?

Ede speaks of his romance with a Master's daughter. Her summer dress and flip-flops … A lily pond … A raft … Skinny-dipping … A bottle of champagne chilling in the water …

Great love will be the making of him, he's sure of it, Ede says. Only romance will teach him what to do with his life.

The bathroom. Guthrie's in the tub, reenacting the death of Seneca under Doyle's direction.

GUTHRIE/SENECA: *As long as you live, keep learning*

how to live; and this is as true for me, today, as it is for any of you. Expectation is the greatest impediment to living; running ahead to tomorrow, it loses today. The day which we fear as our last is but the birthday of eternity ...

How noble Guthrie seems! How profound!

GUTHRIE/SENECA: *Sometimes even to live is an act of courage.*

Guthrie sniffs cocaine from a mirror. Ede rubs some on his gums (it acts more quickly this way, he says). Mulberry, trousers down, applies his cocaine *rectally* (it's even quicker *this* way, he says).

The second bedroom (set aside for ketamine, Mulberry tells us). It's dark inside. The music thumps up from downstairs, bass magnified through the floorboards. Slumped individuals, among them Scroggins ... Is it Scroggins? Yes: there he is, lost in a K-hole.

The third bedroom, Mulberry's, up a second flight of stairs. Posters. Mapplethorpe's men fisting. A large drawing of a headless man, with a labyrinth for viscera and a death's head for genitals, holding a knife in one hand and a bleeding heart in another. A glassed-in roof terrace, full of straggly marijuana plants.

Mulberry laces a spliff with codeine and passes it round. We have to lie down, it's so strong.

The roofs of Cambridge! We're on top of the world! The sky above us. The sky: an abyss. The night: a great cave. What a night to lose our minds!

Benwell is letting off fireworks in the garden. Bursts of colour. Cerise. Vermillion. A Catherine wheel spinning. A smouldering fire, spitting out sparks. Ede says he can *feel* the fireworks. Mulberry says he can *taste* the pink ones.

Three AM. The girls are here. We lie on our bellies,

watching them from the terrace. Girls in Barbour jackets, in vintage fur.

How beautiful the girls are! How beautiful, the fireworks! And we're beautiful, too. All the young are beautiful.

Wittgenstein's brother took his life at *twenty*, we muse. He knew he was all washed up at *twenty*. At our age! And we haven't even *begun* to live! We haven't *done* anything. We haven't *failed* at anything. Our lives lie ahead of us. Wittgenstein says we haven't been *tested* yet, Mulberry reminds us.

To kill yourself at twenty! To have finished with life at twenty! To have run out of options at twenty! Twenty: and for your life to have run its course. To be twenty is surely to be stood at the *brink* of life! To be twenty is yet to have *turned the page*!

Perhaps that's what it means to be brilliant, really brilliant, we speculate: to have already seen past the limits of life. To have seen all the way to the end.

Is that what brilliance means: understanding the whole of life, seeing the whole? Is it that we're not *clever* enough to kill ourselves? We don't *want* to die—not now, not today: is this a sign of our shallowness?

The girls are playing with sparklers. The girls are cooing with delight about their sparklers. How beautiful they are, the girls with their sparklers, making loops in the air ...

They can't help their beauty, we agree. It has nothing to do with them. It has nothing to do with any of us. We are young, so young. But what does our youth *mean*?

A cry from downstairs. Scroggins!

Down we go, forcing our way through the crowds on the staircase. A glimpse of a glassy-eyed Chakrabarti, with a beer backpack and a suction tube. Of Guthrie, snoring on the floor. Both Kirwins in sweaty snogs with Clare College girls.

Then Scroggins, like Kurtz at the end of *Apocalypse Now*. Muttering obscurely. Running his hand over his face. We can't understand what he's saying … The overturning of nonsense … Half words, non-words, speech thickening and wandering and failing …

And then he's out—cold. Locked into his private hell.

Ede googles *ketamine. Causes dissociative anaesthesia,* he reads. That means you can't tell whether you're dreaming or awake, he says. *Ketamine can make you feel you've died and come back to life,* he reads. I'm not sure Scroggins is going to come back to life, I say.

We wave our hands in front of Scroggins's eyes. Nothing. And he smells terrible! Has he soiled himself? Yes! Yes, he has! Scroggins is incontinent!

Mulberry suggests administering MDMA—that'll pick him up. Ede shakes his head. No. It's probably best to call the authorities.

Scroggins is groaning. A deep, abysmal groan. A gurgling in the throat. A kind of living death rattle …

Paramedics come for Scroggins, lifting him onto a stretcher. Would anyone like to accompany him? No! The ambulance rolls off, lights flashing.

Ede and I walk off into the night, to let our heads cool off.

EDE: That girl! That girl! Did you see her?

I shake my head.

EDE (swigging from his bottle): How could you miss her, Peters? She was a dead-ringer for that Cressida—Prince Harry's girl. You know, hippyish. Plaits. Scarf round her hips. Anyway, she's my future wife ... She's Duchess Ede ... (Another swig.) Fuck Scroggins and his emergency. I hope he fucking dies. (A third swig.) Have you ever felt you were *made for something*, Peters? That you had some greater *purpose*? That's what I feel now: I'm made for something. It's all becoming clear. It's to do with that Clare College girl. It's providence. It's *fate*. (Fourth swig.) All the light of the world seemed to rest on her face—did you notice that, Peters?

Ede throws the bottle over a hedge and loses his balance. Ede, flat on his back on the pavement.

He has a faith he never knew he possessed, Ede says. He has *means* he never knew he had ... He feels *taller* than he was.

EDE (sitting up): Am I really taller, Peters?

He's high, he says, as I pull him to his feet. Higher than he's ever been. And it's not drugs. It's life! Life! He's never going to sleep.

He has a sense of the future, he says. Of the *real* future, which is nothing like our present. Tomorrow will not be like today, he says. Tomorrow is going to be quite different from today ...

He's been thrown from the track, Ede says. This is a new direction. He's at the surf's edge. The waves' edge. He won't be afraid to leave himself behind. To relearn everything. He's going to fight against everything he does not love ...

Our College. The staircase to my rooms. Ede gives me some Zs—they'll help you *zzz*, he says. Zolpidem. Zopiclone. Old friends. I swallow a handful, and stagger upstairs.

Class in five hours, I remind myself, setting the alarm clock ...

2

Silence in the classroom.

Mulberry's asleep behind sunglasses. Ede's sunk so low, his head is level with the tabletop. Alexander Kirwin looks vacantly out the window. Benedict Kirwin looks vacantly out the window. Titmuss looks vacantly out the window. Guthrie looks vacantly at Wittgenstein. Chakrabarti just looks vacant. Scroggins, usually the most vacant of all: missing.

The *effort* of thinking. Wittgenstein stands silently in the corner of the room. He grasps his head. He shakes his head. Sweat streams from his face.

Divine help: that's what he needs, he says. We cannot think by ourselves, no more than we can create ourselves.

Wittgenstein asks a general question, and waits for a reply.

Silence.

He asks his question again, slightly rephrasing it.

More silence.

He asks it for a third time.

Still more silence.

Okulu ventures a timorous reply. Wittgenstein waves it aside.

Doyle says something. Not good enough!, Wittgenstein says.

Silence, stretching out. Silence, the equivalent in time to Death Valley. To the Russian steppe. To the surface of the moon ... Oh God, someone say something!

Wittgenstein's silence, his eyes closed, like a man already dead. How *old* he seems! As though he'd read everything and forgotten everything. As though he'd lived not *one* but *several* lives.

His silence. He wants to carry us down, as into the depths of the deepest lake. Like the concrete boots that drag down a body. Down he takes us—into the green depths. He wants to drown us in his depths. But we do not want to be drowned ... We are too *young* to be drowned ...

A walk on the Backs, Wittgenstein walking ahead.

We discuss our most recent hangovers. Mulberry lay in bed for three days. Doyle hallucinated giant spiders dropping from the ceiling. Titmuss heard his name being called by the trees and the flowers. Benedict Kirwin caught the clap. Ede says he's *still* drunk from last weekend. Guthrie's never had a hangover, he says, since he's never stopped drinking. (He's drinking now, sipping from his hip flask.)

Wittgenstein stops. Turns to us.

Five years of philosophy: that's all any of us is good for, he says.

It was all his brother was good for, he says. And now it is five years since his brother's death. Since his brother's *suicide*. Five years in which he, following his brother's example, has *tried* to think ...

Sometimes he wishes he had never begun his studies in logic. His studies in philosophy! Sometimes, he longs for it all to have been a dream. For his logical studies to have been a kind of *fever* ...

To wake up, with his mother's hand on his brow. To wake up, with his brother beside him, in the attic room where they used to sleep—his brother who had likewise never begun his mathematical studies, his *logical* studies; his brother, who had never set out for Oxford, as Wittgenstein had never set out for Cambridge … To wake up, and chatter with his brother about the trees they would climb that day, or the pits they would dig, or the rivers they would ford, or the theatrical sketches they would put on, or the songs they would sing together at the piano, or the dens they would build in the woods, or the birds that would sing above them. To wake up, and speak of anything *but* their studies, anything *but* mathematics, anything *but* logic.

The *Maypole*, after class.

DOYLE: Have you heard? They've had to remove Scroggins's bladder.

EDE: What! Why?

DOYLE: Ketamine damage. After the party.

A shocked pause.

Ede googles *bladder*.

EDE (reading): *The organ that collects urine excreted by the kidneys before disposal by urination.* Can you live without a bladder, do you think?

Ede googles *living without a bladder*.

EDE: They have to find some other way for you to piss. A colostomy bag, or something.

Miserable, we all agree. A bladder is really something you'd miss.

A don in our class; one of the older faculty members. Slippers and blazer, and a pipe poking out of his pocket—do people still smoke pipes? Mug of tea in his hand. How cozy he looks!

Wittgenstein greets him courteously. The don says he'd prefer not to sit on one of the classroom chairs. Doyle goes to get an armchair from the common room, and we move our chairs to make space for it when he returns. The don sits and pulls out a notebook.

Has the don come to steal ideas? To perform some kind of *sabotage*? Is the don letting Wittgenstein know he is being watched? Is the don an infiltrator? A *spy*? Is he preparing a *Wittgenstein dossier* for the authorities?

The don takes notes as Wittgenstein speaks. Meticulous notes. And when the lecture finishes, the don stands to leave. Wittgenstein, catching his eye, gives a little bow. The don bows back.

Afterwards, we walk along the Backs.

The Cambridge trap is closing around him, Wittgenstein says. Good! Let it close! The noose of Cambridge is being tightened round his neck. Good! Let them kick away the stool!

The dons are coming for him, he says. Of course they are! They can sense what he is. They know he comes to *judge* Cambridge. And they know their own time is passing. The time of the don is no more.

• • •

Once, the dons were part of something, Wittgenstein says. Part of the genius of Cambridge, like the ivy on the bridges, like the boathouses along the river. Once, the dons carried the whole history of England on their shoulders, in their processions and their ceremonies—soaring patriotism, a sense of moral purpose, eccentricity, unworldliness, diffidence: resting on the shoulders of the dons.

All of England was once a *lawn*, Wittgenstein says. The whole of the country, with its uplands and lowlands, with its suburbs and towns, was once the *quintessence of lawn*.

The English lawn ran right into the Houses of Parliament. It ran right into Buckingham Palace, into Whitehall and the Law Courts. And into the media empires and the great publishing companies.

The English lawn rolled up to middle-class houses, just as it rolled up to aristocratic mansions. And even if it was halted by working-class concrete, it ran nonetheless through the *heads* of the working classes, just as it ran through the heads of the middle classes and the upper classes—a timeless idea of England.

England has always imagined itself in terms of *rural idyll*, Wittgenstein says. Of the fields' patchwork, all openness and breadth. Of the village green, with its war memorial. Of the parish cemetery, covered with elms. Of pretty little wildernesses, marked off from working land. Of *ornamental* lawns, close-clipped victories over age. Of *informal* lawns, with deer parks and temples. Of *panoramic* lawns, divided only by ha-has. Of *landscaped* lawns, framing the great country houses ...

It was for the green peace of meadow and hedgerow that

English soldiers defended their country from foreign invaders, Wittgenstein says. And it was for the rural idyll they went forth to conquer the world. Wasn't it a simulacrum of the English lawn that they watered in the hill stations of India? Didn't they try to roll out the English lawn in the white mountains of Kenya?

And it was in the name of the English lawn that the *enemy within* was kept down, Wittgenstein says. The Peasants' Revolt was crushed for seeking equality on the English lawn. The Diggers were transported for declaring that the English lawn was part of the commons. And the new industrialists sent their sons to become *good little gentlemen* in the public schools of the English lawn.

But never was the English lawn so lush as in the *great universities of England!*, Wittgenstein says. Old expanses of lawn, strewn with meadowsweet and buttercups in high summer. Crocuses blooming in spring. Students picnicking, all white-flannelled elegance.

And the old dons, of the *great universities of England*— the English lawn ran through their hearts, Wittgenstein says. The old dons lived out their lives on the English lawn. They sipped warm beer and watched cricket on the English lawn. They munched crustless sandwiches at garden parties on the English lawn. And one day, they were *laid to rest* in the English lawn.

The dons drew all their strength from the English lawn, Wittgenstein says. They were always *sure of things* on the English lawn. You could never *best* a don on the English lawn. You would only *break your lance* tilting at a don on the English lawn.

Of course, the English lawn was ultimately *provincial,*

Wittgenstein says. The philosophy of the English lawn was concerned exclusively with *English lawn issues*, which is to say with nothing of any real importance. Nothing really *mattered* in English-lawn philosophy, he says. Nothing was really *at stake* in English-lawn thought. The don was a *lawn-head*! No more than a lawn-head!

But perhaps there was *something* to the world of the dons, Wittgenstein says. Perhaps there was something to be said for donnish amateurism, for donnish pottering-about. Perhaps there was a value to pass-the-port philosophy. To home-counties philosophy! Perhaps there was a *freedom* to the English don—no German stuffiness, no French pretension ...

The old world! The old dons! The old lawn—spreading into the distance! The old dream of a Jerusalem to be built on England's green and pleasant land!

The English lawn is receding, Wittgenstein says. And with it, the world of the old dons of Cambridge.

New housing estates, where once was open countryside ... A new science park where once were allotments and orchards ... New apartment blocks near the station, their balconies in shade ... And towering barbarisms: Varsity Hotel, looming over Park Parade; Botanic House, destroying the Botanic Gardens; Riverside Place, desecrating the River Cam ...

They're *developing* the English lawn, Wittgenstein says. They're building glassy towers on the English lawn. They're laying out suburbs and exurbs on the English lawn. They're developing new business parks on the English lawn. They're constructing Megalopolis on the English lawn.

And they're developing the English *head*, Wittgenstein

says. They're building glass-and-steel towers in the English *head*. They're building suburbs and exurbs in the English *head* ...

The new don is nothing but a *suburb-head*, Wittgenstein says. The new don—bidding for funds, *exploring synergies with industry*, looking for *corporate sponsorship*, launching *spin-off companies*. The new don, courting venture capitalists, seeking business partners, looking to *export the Cambridge brand*. The new don—with a *head full of concrete*. A finance-head. A capitalist-head.

Do we believe the dons *teach* at Cambridge? No, they *train* at Cambridge! Do we believe the dons *think* at Cambridge? No, they *bid* at Cambridge! They *network*. They grub about for money. They ride the waves of global finance.

The new don has sold his soul!, Wittgenstein says. The new don has sold his university! The new don has *monetised* Cambridge! The new don has made Cambridge into an *advert*.

It was the new dons who made Oxford unbearable for his brother, Wittgenstein says. The new-style philosophers!

English philosophy has become *business* philosophy, *grant-chasing* philosophy, his brother told him. The Oxford philosophy department dreams only of being *Big Philosophy*, his brother said. Of founding Philosophy Parks, of donning philosophical lab coats ...

There are Oxford chairs in the *desecration* of philosophy, his brother told him. In the *murder* of philosophy. In the *destruction* of philosophy. In the *strangulation* of philosophy.

His brother overheard a don use the phrase *learning competencies*, Wittgenstein says. His brother was asked to demonstrate the *real-world applicability* of his fundamental work in logic. His brother was expected to make a case for the *impact* of his thought on the world at large.

His brother said nothing, Wittgenstein says. He kept mute. But he knew he had to leave the high table, and to leave Oxford. He knew he had no choice but to *leave England*.

Almost all of us have liaisons. Brief encounters, lasting no more than a night. But *relationships*—no, not really. Never anything that serious. There is never anything that serious at Cambridge. The Cambridge years don't count. They're years out, years on holiday. *Frivolous* years, not part of ordinary life. Cambridge is just a playground ...

Brief encounters ... One-night stands ... One-week flings ... One-term relationships ... But *romance?* Romance has nothing to do with us.

A one-nighter—snog in a club, home in a taxi, pulling off clothes, opening a condom packet, a study-bedroom fuck, bed rocking, bed creaking, staggering home in the dawn. A whole weekend—lying in bed and doing it again, and then again and again. As long as a fortnight—as long as infatuation surges through us, until, one day, lust gets bored, yawns and stretches its limbs ...

But Ede's love for Phaedra (Fee) is entirely different, he says.

He tracked her down, he says. He found her at some dreadful rah birthday party.

Raves are full of posh girls now, waving glowsticks and going all trippy, he says. And the DJs have double-barrelled names.

And there she was, in the middle of it all, Ede says. The sum of all beauty. The centre of the world.

EDE: Do you know what it means to dance, Peters? To really move?

He danced, Ede says. He broke out his moves. He mouthed song lyrics. He acted them out. He was slick. He was funny. She laughed. He smiled. He mouthed, *I like you.* She looked demure. He mouthed, *Shall we go outside?* She mouthed, *Yes.*

Outside into the cool clear night. Fee: the centre of the world. And he, beside Fee, close to the centre. The pair of them, carving out their little channel in space-time.

Everything is true, he thought to himself, as they walked. *The stars are hard and bright and true. The moon is true. The night is true . . .*

Remember this, he thought to himself. *I am awake and the world is new. Life is alive in me. Life is alive in a new way.*

Does she know how beautiful she is?, he thought to himself. *She's Guinevere. She's Helen of Troy. Wars could be fought over her. Murders committed. Holy vows broken.*

I should kneel, he thought to himself. *I should fall to my knees. I have been called, like a prophet. I have been chosen. I have a mission. The bells of life are ringing in my ears.*

It was as if the world was rocking, Ede says. His knees were weak. To walk was to stagger. The pavement was a ladder mounting upwards.

He laid his coat on her shoulders. She nestled into him. *I am Certainty*, he thought to himself. *I am Protection. I am the Firm Ground.* And her heart was the fluttering bird that he wanted to stalk, to catch, to hold, to free . . .

And later that night, he bared her upper body. Later, he saw her white skin, her breasts, her luminous face, full of everything divine . . .

Wittgenstein is hoarse this morning. He pulls a tube of cough sweets from his jacket pocket. He unwraps one, and pops it into his mouth.

He speaks of the *undoing* of logic. Of logic's *deactivation*. He speaks of the *release* of logic, as of captive birds into the wild.

He speaks of giving logic a kind of *freedom*. A kind of *wildness*. He speaks of *unfettering* logic. Of taking off logic's blinkers. He speaks of letting logic soar up wildly into its own sky ...

Logic is lost, that's the trouble, he says. Logic has got lost. We must lead logic back to itself, he says. We must let logic recover its memories.

And one day, logic will whisper in our ears, he says. Logic will say the kindest words. We will mistake it for roaring, he says. We will confuse it with the howling wind ...

And logic will bloom in our hearts, he says. And then we'll see it—that our hearts, all along, were *logical* hearts. And logic, which we think we master, will be *our* master, he says. Logic will be the crown we wear on our heads ...

Redemption: that's what he seeks. Logical redemption. Logical *love*. It must sound strange to speak of logical *love*. But there really is such a thing as logical *love*.

It must sound strange to speak of the *blood* of logic, he says. Of the *heart* of logic. But there really is such a thing as the *blood* of logic. As the *heart* of logic.

In his dream, the *Logik* is light, he says. The *Logik* laughs.

In his dream, the *Logik* can be expressed in a single greeting. In a single *word*. In his dream, the whole of the *Logik* can be expressed in a gesture. In a handshake. In a friendly nod of the head.

A walk in Grantchester, under the weak winter sun. Wittgenstein, in a terrible mood. Whose idea was this?, he demands.

Over the centuries, the academics of Cambridge have *worn a path* to Grantchester, he says. Over the centuries, the academics of Cambridge have sought to *cool off their minds* in the willow-shade of Grantchester. To *slip down a few gears* on the river-path to Grantchester. The Grantchester walk was part of the *rhythm* of their work; the *respiration* of their work. The Grantchester walk let their work *breathe*. The Grantchester walk *expired* in their work.

It's the very opposite for him, he says, as we walk along the river. His work *suffocates* from the Grantchester walk. His work becomes increasingly *airless* as a result of the Grantchester walk. He might as well *place a plastic bag over the head of his work* as take the Grantchester walk. He might as well *place a plastic bag over his own head* as take the Grantchester walk!

Leaving Cambridge for Grantchester means you have to return to Cambridge, he says. The walk to Grantchester and back is still in the orbit of Cambridge. In Grantchester, there is still the dreadful *gravitational pull* of Cambridge. The dreadful *tractor-beam* of Cambridge. Cambridge still calls you back. Cambridge still waits for you, laughing at you. *You thought you could escape me? You thought you could get away?*

In the end, the walk to Grantchester is only a way to *pace the floor of his cell*, he says. As indeed any trip from Cambridge is only a way to *pace the floor of your cell*. A trip to London from Cambridge is only a way to *pace the floor of your cell*. A trip to

Norwich from Cambridge is only another way to *pace the floor of your cell*. A trip to Ely Cathedral—just another way to *pace the floor of your cell*.

To leave Cambridge is to *return* to Cambridge. To try to escape Cambridge is only to be more *imprisoned* in Cambridge. Cambridge!, he exclaims. Grantchester!, he exclaims. Cambridge! Grantchester! The path to Grantchester! The path to Cambridge! The path to Grantchester is only ever the path to Cambridge!

Byron's Pool. The famous willows, the famous swans, the famous reeds. The concrete weir must be a new addition.

Byron bathed here with his pet bear, we read on a plaque. And Rupert Brooke and the neo-pagans, a century later. And Augustus John came with his gypsy wagon and his clutch of sun-browned children ...

Signs everywhere. Explaining Byron's Pool. Explaining Byron. Explaining Rupert Brooke and Augustus John. Explaining the trees. Explaining the wildlife. Explaining the *green and blue corridor* through Cambridge—the proposed cycle path and the planned BMX track.

Why must everything be explained?, Wittgenstein asks. As soon as there are signs about trees, there are no trees. As soon as there are information boards about wildlife, there is no wildlife. As soon as there's a Byron plaque and an Augustus John plaque and a Rupert Brooke plaque, the legacies of Byron and Augustus John and Rupert Brooke are *entirely destroyed*. As soon as there's a plaque explaining Grantchester, Grantchester itself is *wiped from the face of the earth*.

But perhaps that's no bad thing, he says: wiping Grantchester from the face of the earth.

· · ·

He has *insomnia*, he says. Terrible shrieks wake him at night. Screams—which should say, *I am being murdered! Help me at once!* But which in fact say, *I am drunk! My head is empty!* Cries—which should be those of dying men, mortally wounded men, lying in no-man's-land or beneath collapsed buildings, but which are really the voices of students ...

Students, bellowing on their phones. Great, health-filled, stupid voices, booming out. Stupidity, echoing from the ancient walls. Stupidity, sounding through his rooms. Stupidity, shrieking through the hollow night.

He can't work, Wittgenstein says. He can't write.

His powers are failing, he says. What presumption even to *speak* of his powers!

To begin—that would be enough. To take a single step forward. To discover a starting point that does not give way ... Why do the foundations of his thought always crumble? Why does the path of his reflections always peter out?

WITTGENSTEIN: The *will* to work is wearing me out. But not the work itself.

He speaks of the *joy* of work. Of the *bliss* of work, and of *honest exhaustion* after a whole day of work. He speaks of the Sabbath of God, of the seventh day of creation. He speaks of the Saturday that does not set.

How will he find his way to the eye of the logical storm?, he asks. When will everything become clear? When will it stay still? The heart of logic is terribly calm, he says. True peace, for him, is really logical peace.

Mulberry and Doyle's spat.

EDE: How did it start?

MULBERRY: He wrote *wide arse* in Greek on my door.

EDE: But didn't you write *I will fuck both your arses and your mouths* in Latin on *his* door?

MULBERRY: I was quoting Catullus!

EDE: *He* was quoting Aristophanes.

MULBERRY. Well, he felt-tipped *very cheap whore* in Greek on my door.

EDE: But you marker-penned *hung like a Chihuahua* on *his* door. In English, so everyone could read it! Where's that from, anyway—Sophocles? (A pause.) There's a frisson between the pair of you, anyone can see it. It's like an electric storm.

Mulberry likes that, he says: an electric storm. It turns him on.

EDE: Everything turns you on, Mulberry. But I do wish you and Doyle would settle things. All this tension's getting wearing.

Wittgenstein's questions!

Is it actually the case that ... ?; Would you consider it impor-tant to ... ?; Is it, in this instance, really worth considering ... ?; Are we entitled to draw the conclusion that ... ?; Would we be entirely in error to ... ?

Doesn't he understand that we do not *dwell* with these is-sues as he does? That they do not exercise our thoughts night and day, as they do his?

It would be alright if he didn't expect us to understand him. If we didn't *need* to understand him. If he simply thought *for* us, in our place. If he simply presented a *spectacle*—of what it means to think, of what it means to take thought seriously.

No one expects very much of an undergraduate: he should know that. None of us will fail our degrees, it is true—no one fails anymore. But none of us will excel, either. We're here to fill the classrooms, and pay the fees. We're here to populate the corridors, and sit decorously on the steps.

What does it matter what *we* think?

His questions!

Might it not also be the case that ... ?; Is it worth admitting the possibility that ... ?

Doesn't he understand we just want to *get things right*? To *do well*? To get *high marks*? The rest, all of philosophy, doesn't really matter ...

But he demands our attention. He addresses us directly. *Okulu, what do you understand by this? Doyle, can you think of a way out of this apparent dilemma?*

He asks us the kinds of questions that he would ask himself. Questions beyond our understanding. Questions that soar above us. Questions that graze the philosophical sky ... We try to answer, but how can we? We stumble. We stutter. We say silly things. But what else does he expect?

Wittgenstein does not hide his derision.

He knows the Cambridge student is encouraged to talk, he says. He knows the Cambridge student is to be treated as an intellectual partner, even as an intellectual *equal*, he says. He knows he's supposed to take heed of whatever nonsense the Cambridge student utters. He knows he's supposed to say *interesting* to even the most fatuous point.

He knows he's supposed to glory in the very fact that we *can* speak, that we say anything at all, that we've even turned up for class, he says. He knows he's supposed to *clap his hands in delight*, that the Cambridge student has deigned to add his voice to the *great tradition of philosophy*.

He knows he's supposed to fall upon the most trivial comment as though it were uttered by *Immanuel Kant*, he says. He knows he's supposed to nod seriously to every word that drops from our lips, as though it were *Kant himself* who was speaking. He knows all this, he says.

He watches our faces, he says. He looks for signs of understanding. But what does he see? Nothing! Nothing!

What do we know of the struggle to think? What, when everything has come to us so easily? That's how he sees us, he says: as those to whom everything has come easily.

What do we know of the desire to think? Of the *love* of wisdom?

Perhaps we are simply too *young* for philosophy, he says. Too blithe. We haven't yet run up against *life's difficulties*, he says. Against the *tragedy of life*. You can see that in our faces, he says. We know nothing of *life's calamities*—of madness, suicide, all that.

In a sense, our indifference to philosophy is a kind of *liberation*, he says. It is lightness itself. We do not know the *gravity* of thought. We feel no philosophical weight. We walk like astronauts on the moon, in great blithe leaps, in huge bounds. Nothing keeps us to the surface of our studies. Nothing holds us down.

Once, it was possible to learn things, and to be shaped by your learning, he says. Once, to be a student meant to be *formed* by what you learned. To let it enter your soul. But today?

We're drowning in openness, he says. In our sense of the possible. We're ready to take anything in—to learn about anything, and therefore about *nothing*. Everything is available to us, and therefore *nothing* is available to us. Everything is at our disposal, and therefore *nothing* is at our disposal. We are infinitely open-minded, which is to say, infinitely *closed*-minded.

Our sense of our own *potential*—he sees it in us. Our sense of our *youth*. Our belief that the world lies *open before us*. Don't we understand that it is our very sense of *potential* that is the problem? That it is our very sense of *youth* that is the problem? That it is our sense that the world *lies open before us* that is the problem?

• • •

There was a time when learning awoke unknown desires, he says. Desires for what lay outside you, outside your grasp.

There was a time when students knew how to *reach*, and that they had to reach.

And now? Before our desires even coalesce, they are answered. Before our desires become desires, they are satisfied. Our desires are met before we even have them.

There's no yearning, for us. No sense that something lies beyond.

Joy, joy, joy, tears of joy: that's what Pascal had inscribed on his posthumous memorial, Wittgenstein says. Those who know nothing of grief can know nothing of joy, either.

Ede, hand in the air. Wittgenstein ignores him.

He knows how we live, he says. He knows how we *do not live*.

Drinking doubles and trebles at bars in which we cannot hear ourselves speak. Drinking doubles and trebles because we have *absolutely nothing to say* to one another.

We drink because we do not live, he says. Because we have no idea what it means to live.

He's heard the thump-thump of our music. He's heard our drunken laughter.

We're guzzlers, he says. Devourers. Cambridge is a trough, and we are its pigs.

How disgusting we are! How *filthy*—morally speaking! *Actually* speaking.

We're stupid, he says. Shallow. We're without soul. Without *insight*.

Do we *know* it?, he wonders. Do we have any idea of it? Do we *sense* what we lack? Do we understand that life's seriousness lies far beyond us? Is that why we drink ourselves into insensibility? Why we *deaden* ourselves? Is that why we half destroy ourselves, and leave the contents of our stomachs on the courtyard flagstones?

No, we have no sense of what we lack, he says. Life's seriousness means nothing to us.

Pints of Weissbier in the *Free Press*.

KIRWIN A: Why does Wittgenstein think we're such idiots? We got into Cambridge, for fuck's sake! That's got to count for something.

MULBERRY: Well—*he's* obviously suffered for his thought. Now it's *our* turn.

KIRWIN B: But why should we bother to suffer? It's not as if he's a great *advert* for the philosophical life.

ME: Maybe we *are* a bit too proud. Or stupid. Or whatever else it is he says. Maybe we *do* need some discipline.

EDE: You, Peters, are a masochist. I don't mean a sexual masochist. You're a *thought* masochist, which is much worse.

MULBERRY: Peters thinks Wittgenstein is our very own genius. I've seen the way you look at him, Peters! Like a swooning schoolgirl!

ME: And what if he *is* a genius?

KIRWIN A: I don't know … I think it's all theatre, all smoke and mirrors.

MULBERRY: It probably takes a genius to know a genius. Otherwise, it's just blind faith.

ME: Then *I* have faith. We all do—why else do we come to class?

KIRWIN B: To watch a nervous breakdown, that's why. A slo-mo nervous collapse. We're voyeurs.

EDE: No—we come to class to try to discover why it is we continue to come to class.

KIRWIN A: Oh, very fucking clever, Ede.

Benwell's mutiny.

Wittgenstein wants to become a kind of *mirror* for us, he says. A mirror in which we can see the shortcomings of our own thinking. Of our own temptations of thought. Of our own *philosophical temptations*.

Benwell, clicking and unclicking his pen. Benwell, tutting. Shuffling his papers.

BENWELL (interrupting): This is all nonsense! None of this means anything!

Wittgenstein looks at him calmly.

BENWELL: I'm tired of all this posh boy SHITE.

DOYLE: Do shut up, Benwell!

BENWELL (to Doyle): Don't you fucking start!

DOYLE: Start what?

The Kirwins stir menacingly in their seats.

BENWELL (leaving): Fuck the lot of you.

The *Maypole*, after class.

Benwell's going to kill us all, Doyle says, he's sure of it.

Ede says he'd quite like to be poor and northern, and full of bitterness. He'd start a band. He'd sing about being poor and northern, and full of bitterness ...

Discussion of Benwell. Is it just that Benwell is very, very bad at doing good, or is his evil something real, like Voldemort, or something? Was Benwell always evil? Was he an evil child? An evil five-year-old? At what point did Benwell become evil? When did Benwell go over to the dark side?

Or is it just that Benwell's poor (Ede's view)? A victim of the class system (Ede again)? Is it that Benwell's had none of the advantages of the rest of us, even Peters (Ede)? Is it that Benwell will only come into his own after the revolution (Ede, for a final time)?

In Doyle's rooms, before the Pembroke College toga party. We've each brought a bottle of white spirits, as instructed: vodka, gin, tequila, Bacardi. Doyle mixes them up with pastis and coke. The Black Zombie: Doyle's favourite tipple.

A performance of the death of Socrates, inspired by David's painting. Guthrie as Socrates, sitting upright on the bed, one hand gesturing wildly, the other reaching out for the cup that Ede passes him. The rest of us as Socrates's followers, our eyes full of tears.

Guthrie looks so *dignified*, we all agree. Guthrie is fully believable, reaching out for the cup of hemlock/Black Zombie the jurists of Athens had condemned him to drink—his sentence for corrupting the young. The real Socrates drained the cup willingly, claiming that there was nothing for the philosopher to fear in death.

GUTHRIE/SOCRATES: *Give me the hemlock, jailer! For I am unafraid of death, as all philosophers should be.* (Turning to us.) *And you lot, stop your weeping! Cease your lamentations! What a display you make of yourselves! Don't you know dying is something to be done in silence!*

Guthrie drains the cup without flinching. He falls to the ground. Ede (playing the part of Phaedo) closes Guthrie's eyes.

EDE/PHAEDO: *Truly we have lost the best of the men of Athens, the wisest! The most just!*

Applause from everyone. Guthrie rises, grinning like a fool. Another round of Black Zombies. Toasts to Socrates! To Plato! To the eternal soul! To Beauty as such and in general! To the sun! To the Greeks! To philosophy!

MULBERRY: To homosexuality!

Have we ever wondered why all the Greek philosophers were gay?, Mulberry asks. It was a hangover from the ancient warrior cult: the older man takes a younger one as both tutee and lover. You learned, you fucked, you fucked, you learned. And the ones who learned most (and fucked most) became philosophers.

Mulberry says he hasn't learnt anything from fucking. And he hasn't taught anything either. Quite the opposite, in fact.

The Greeks spoke of ascending the erotic ladder, Mulberry says. Of moving from the love of beautiful boys to the love of beautiful forms in nature, to the love of mathematical laws, to the love of beauty itself...

For his part, Mulberry's *descending* the erotic ladder, he says. Love has no lessons for him, he says. He's going all the way down to the abyss. All the way to hell, to brimstone and black flames.

Mulberry riding bareback, and boasting of riding bareback... Mulberry, courting death. Asking for it... Mulberry toying with death, because he wants *it* to toy with *him*. He wants death to wrestle him down, to hold him down. He wants to take death itself as his lover, he says, to be loved by death, all the way to death. For death's black lips to kiss his own.

Mulberry speaks of the desire for death to explore him with its tendrils. For death to reach into his mouth. His arsehole. He speaks of his desire to take death into his body. For *real* death to free him from the *desire* for death. For death to stir him, wake him, return him to life... For death to grow inside him, a dark flower... For death to open its fist inside him... For death to flume up, black. For death to fill his sky.

Now death is all round him, black, roaring, and he is tiny. Now death is the black hole that swallowed the sky. Now death's black pupils are looking into his. Now death's dark mouth is laughing in his own ...

General amusement. Black Zombies bring out the Mephistopheles in Mulberry.

The phases of Guthrie's drunkenness. Amiability. A smiling be-toga-ed Guthrie, sitting with an arm round his be-toga-ed neighbour. Guthrie, nodding and laughing. Guthrie, all hail-fellow-well-met. Guthrie, buying round after round at the bar. Guthrie, flush-faced and cheery. Guthrie, full of smiles and bonhomie.

Then excitability, barely containable. Euphoric Guthrie, keen to stay out and never go home. Guthrie, still dancing as the house lights come on. Red-eyed Guthrie singing in the streets on the way home. Guthrie, juggling. Guthrie, walking on his hands. What *life* there is in Guthrie! Guthrie, inexhaustible! Guthrie, bubbling over!

Then, frenzied drinking. Guthrie, his face glowing. His eyes staring maniacally. Guthrie, trembling, laughing wildly. Guthrie, becoming mad. Becoming *animal*! Guthrie, wanting more, even when the bar's already closed. *More!* Guthrie, pointing accusatory fingers. Guthrie, declaring war on each of us. Guthrie, dealing out insults. Guthrie, promising revenge. Guthrie, telling us we'll all come to dreadful ends. Guthrie, speaking of judgement and deserved punishment. Guthrie, taking himself for an avenging angel. Guthrie, swiping at us, missing, knocking pint glasses onto the floor ...

Then Guthrie calming down, on the walk home. Guthrie, waxing philosophical. Quoting Heraclitus, reaching back into the origins of European thought: *the way up is the way down!* Shouting out the one word we have left from Anaximander:

aperion! Quoting Thales in Greek and then in English: *everything is water!* Lying on the green grass of the quad, whispering of the great tragedies of antiquity. Of the story of the Persian defeat at Salamis. Of the horrors of the siege of Hadrianopolis. Guthrie, taking the part of Antigone addressing Creon; of Oedipus, addressing the gods. How poignant he is! How moving!

Guthrie, his head falling back. Guthrie, asleep amidst the flowers, snoring loudly. Guthrie, unconscious in the mud, his toga undone.

DOYLE (pointing): What the fuck is that?

EDE: Guthrie's third nipple.

DOYLE: Why is it so *hairy*?

Ede googles *third nipple*.

EDE: *Supernumerary nipples.* They can grow anywhere on the body, apparently.

MULBERRY: For example you, Doyle, are nothing but a supernumerary nipple.

Once upon a time, Guthrie would have been burnt as a witch, we agree. Then again, he might have been revered as a seer ... Does a third nipple give you second sight?, we wonder. It's a *sign*, at any rate, we agree. Guthrie's been chosen! But for what?

We should start a new religion, we agree, with Guthrie as our mock king, our Lord of Misrule, at the head of the feast. We should crown Guthrie as our Bacchus, our Pan ...

A final toast to Guthrie and his third nipple, as the day begins around us. Doors slam and showers steam. Students' footsteps on the stairs. Students pouring into the courtyard, heading to lectures.

Jesus Green, after class.

Wittgenstein is certain that he is in *immediate physical danger* in Cambridge, he says. That he will be stabbed by a poisoned umbrella tip, like a spy. That he will be bitten by a mad dog. A mad *Labrador*. He is certain that a gust of wind will blow him into the River Cam. He is certain that he will be *driven to suicide* by the dons.

His brother warned him that it was only a matter of time before the dons expelled him from Cambridge. The only question was how long he could work unnoticed. Because if they found out what he was working on—*really* working on—they'd get rid of him in an instant.

His brother told him to see himself as an *illicit* thinker, Wittgenstein says. As a secret scholar. There was his ostensible work, concerned with *metatheoretic reasoning* and *idempotence*, on which he would no doubt publish a few articles, which he would discuss at a few learned symposia, Wittgenstein says. And then there was his *real* work, of which he must tell no one, his brother advised. Work only for after hours, when everyone is asleep. There was the work he'd told the Cambridge dons he'd come to the university to do; and there was his *real* work, of which he should say nothing to the dons ...

If the dons only knew of their secret work!, his brother said. If they only knew where their *fundamental work in philosophical logic* was leading them! If they only knew that their logical project could only mean the *destruction* of Oxford, of Cambridge, of the dons, of it all!

• • •

We stop by the duck pond.

His brother warned him about the dons, Wittgenstein says. *Don't trust them!*, his brother said. *Keep an eye on them!*

The dons of Cambridge would be his warders, his brother said. His prison guards. (Just as the dons of Oxford were *his* warders, *his* prison guards.) Oh, they'd seem very gentle; they'd seem to be the easiest-going people he could find. They'd be full of *soft skills*, the dons of Cambridge (just like the dons of Oxford). They'd be full of *words of kindness*. But that would be when they were at their most deadly, his brother warned: when they were speaking *words of kindness*.

He shouldn't be fooled by a smiling don, his brother told him. He shouldn't allow himself to be *lulled* by a don. *Charmed* by one. He should never get too *close* to a don, his brother said. Never allow himself to be *befriended*. He shouldn't *take tea* with a don, or join a don at the high table, his brother said. There should be no after-dinner drinks with a don. No *evening constitutionals*.

He should *isolate* himself, his brother said. He should become an *island*. Turn up for events to which he was required to turn up; speak when he was expected to speak, and leave it at that. Render unto Caesar the things of Caesar, and keep his soul for his work.

His brother spoke of the *danger* of the dons, Wittgenstein says. Of the *threat* of the dons. Dons were more dangerous than they seemed, his brother said. Dons could *go for the throat*, his brother was sure of that.

His brother had heard of scenes of savagery among the dons. Scenes of *violence*. Whole packs of dons would go out to hunt, in the guest lectures and seminar series of Oxford. Don-packs, out to bring back meat to feast upon.

He'd seen them in his mind's eye, his brother said: great dons, like lions, chewing on bones; lesser dons, like hyenas, sucking on the bones left by other dons; still lesser dons, like birds of prey, flapping round the corpse ...

Of course, dons could be *gentle*, too, his brother acknowledged. Dons could be tender, even *kind*. When they first scented spring in the air, dons would become dreamy and sentimental. When the first spring breezes ruffled their hair, dons would close their eyes and *sigh* ...

In the high summer, dons would sit out on the grass like resting lions, his brother said. They'd picnic on the lawn, like kings at peace. They'd recline in their deckchairs, laying their Loeb editions facedown on the grass.

Autumn lent the dons a *valedictory* air, his brother said. In autumn, when the first leaves were falling from the trees, the dons would know a gentle melancholy. Sometimes a tear would appear in the eye of a melancholic don. Sometimes a don would let out a great sigh, as he sat in his leather armchair by the fire.

In winter, the dons were inert, eyes glazed over, his brother said. Drowsy, like a winter wasp. Half hibernating by the fire, a glass of sherry in the hand ...

But he should never be fooled, his brother told him. He should never let down his guard.

The mood of the dons could change quickly, his brother said. Like a bushfire that suddenly changes direction. You couldn't predict them. You couldn't anticipate them. Their moods were unstable. They were easy to stir, easy to panic. They were susceptible to rumour, to gossip. They were as sensitive as antelopes. A sudden movement, and they'd bolt—a herd of dons leaping over the savannah.

Above all, he should never show *fear* to a don, his brother said. He might be afraid of them, but he should never show his fear. That's what his brother had learnt. The best thing would be for the dons to take him as one of their own. As a kind of *honorary* don, an honorary fellow. He should try, as best he could, to *mirror* the dons. His brother advised him to ape their gestures, their turns of phrase. To mimic their body language. Their *dress*. To try to *blend in* with the dons—they'd appreciate that.

Of course, not for one moment would they take him for a don—they would not be so easily fooled, his brother said. Not for one moment would they take him for one of their kind. But they'd appreciate the *gesture* of his would-be donnishness. They'd smile when they witnessed his no-doubt inept attempts at becoming a don. It would be as though he were a child, playing at dressing up, his brother said. And the dons, despite everything, are fond of children ...

Doyle's rooms. A soirée.

Tonight's performance: the madness of Nietzsche.

Guthrie, the star, is unconscious. Doyle smears mustard under his nostrils. No response. Doyle squirts wasabi through his lips. Still nothing. Titmuss volunteers for the part, and sellotapes a moustache under his nose.

Titmuss/Nietzsche's last moments of sanity, watching a horse (Benedict Kirwin) being beaten in the Turin marketplace. Titmuss/Nietzsche, flinging his arms round the horse, and weeping.

TITMUSS/NIETZSCHE: *You must have chaos inside you, if you are to give birth to a dancing star. What doesn't kill you makes you stronger. When you look into an abyss, the abyss also looks into you.*

Titmuss/Nietzsche slumps. Applause from the audience.

Change of scene.

The demented Nietzsche never regained consciousness, Doyle says. Everyone ponders Guthrie.

EDE: He's actually drooling.

MULBERRY: You go, Guthrie! Give an Oscar to droolio!

Guthrie has something, we agree. Presence. He's like an Olivier of the immobile. Even his inertia is profound. As though he bore all the weight of existence! All the burden of being!

DOYLE (playing Nietzsche's sister): Friedrich! Friedrich! Wake up!

Guthrie half snores. Sniffs.

DOYLE/NIETZSCHE'S SISTER: Friedrich! Herr Hitler has come to see you!

Guthrie seems to stir. His eyes half open. Then his head slumps onto his chest.

More applause. Doyle bows. A triumph! Bravo!

Black Zombies all round.

TITMUSS: Do you reckon you have to be *mad* to really think?

MULBERRY: Wittgenstein's mad. Quite clearly.

EDE: Wittgenstein's brother *went* mad. Then killed himself.

DOYLE: It must run in the family.

EDE: I had a mad uncle.

MULBERRY: Mad uncle Ede—must be from all that inbreeding. Did *he really think*?

EDE: I don't know. He really thought he was a parrot. Or a squirrel, depending on the day.

Another round of Zombies.

Spin the bottle.

The usual questions: Ever done it out-of-doors? Anally? With a member of the same sex? The opposite sex? Favourite sexual fantasies?: the secretary (Chakrabarti) … the nurse (Titmuss) … the dominant woman (Alexander Kirwin) … the virgin flower, atremble in your arms (Benedict Kirwin), the threesome (Benedict Kirwin again), the *foursome* (Benedict Kirwin yet again), a *Roman orgy* of women (Benedict Kirwin has a lot of fantasies) …

MULBERRY: No prizes for guessing *your* fantasy, Peters.

EDE: Yeah. Germanic genius all dressed up in *leder*.

The Kirwins are quizzed about their brief encounters at the *derangement of the senses* party. Mulberry is quizzed about the ethics of *riding bareback*. About the sex/death relationship. We explore the topics of fisting, of auto-erotic asphyxiation. We discuss the effects of various drugs on sexual performance. On methods of relaxing the anal sphincter (Mulberry). Of engorging the reluctant cock (Doyle).

We rank the company in terms of sexual promiscuity (Mulberry wins). In terms of sexual *prowess* (Titmuss claims to be an expert in the Indian erotic arts. No one believes him). In terms of sexual *attractiveness*, Ede comes top (centuries of breeding). In terms of *sexual repression*.

MULBERRY: You win that one, Peters. Hands down.

Saturday night. Ede texts. *You up? I split with Fee.*

Ede, in the communal kitchen, emptying a tub of mushrooms onto the counter.

EDE: The best I could get. Guaranteed head-fuck.

Fee! Fee! Why must it all be so complicated?, Ede says. We're cursed. We're *doomed.*

Beauty seems like a great clue, Ede says. Plato was right. It points somewhere. But to what? There is *this* world, that is all. Beauty makes a sign—but of what? A sign of nothing. Of the absence of signs. Beauty mocks us, Ede says. Beauty says: *The way is barred. There is no path.* Beauty is the door that's shut.

Fee! Fee! It's unbearable, Ede says. He can't stand it! Fee is beautiful, but Fee is witless. Fee and her friends: beautiful but witless, chattering away in their flat. So inane. So depthless.

EDE: Have you noticed how the rahs are all saying *literally* now? *I was like literally exhausted. I was like literally wasted.* But nothing they say actually *means* anything! Literally *or* figuratively! Most of the time, they don't even finish their sentences. *I was literally so* . . . They just trail off. They barely *speak*, most of the time. *Mmm*s and *ahh*s. Little moans, nothing else. *Oh reeealllly. Lurrrrrvely. Coooool.*

And they use the word *uni*, which is unforgiveable, Ede says. *My uni* . . . As if Cambridge were some cuddly toy. As if *they* were all cuddly toys.

He's known these people all his life, Ede says. He's supposed to marry one of them! To perpetuate the breed. To join one great house with another, consolidating landed wealth, and so on. Fee would do perfectly, he says. He was led to her, it is quite clear, by some *innate aristocratic homing device.* Something *Darwinian.* Something quite disgusting ...

EDE: We're puppets, Peters!

Better to ruin himself, Ede says. Better to ruin the whole Ede legacy. To squander its fortune. To wreck its great estates. Better to end the family line. Better to become a cautionary tale to scare young aristocrats, he says.

Ede steeps the mushrooms in warm water, adding a squeeze of lemon juice. We drink the tea.

We speak of our desire for despair—real despair, Ede and I. For choking despair, visible to all. For chaotic despair, despair of *collapse*, of *ruination*. For the despair of Lucifer, as he fell from heaven ...

Our desire for *annulling* despair. For a despair that dissolves the ego; despair indistinguishable from a kind of *death*. For *wild* despair, for heads thrown back, teeth fringing laughing mouths. For *exhilarated* despair, for madness under the moon.

Our desire for despairs of the damned. For *crawling* despairs, like rats, like spiders. For *heavy* despairs, like those on vast planets, which make a teardrop as heavy as lead ...

Our desire for the moon to smash into the earth. For the sun to swallow the earth. For the night to devour both the sun and the earth.

We speak of our desire for extinction, for cool mineral silence. For the Big Crunch, for the end of all things. For the Great Dissipation, when electrons leave their atoms ...

Our desire for the right to exist to be revoked. For the great lie of life to lose its force. For all to end in the great Beckett-play of the end ...

We speak of our desire for the universal wind-down. For our bubble universe to pop on the mouth of God-the-idiot. For the great going-under. For the death of death of death. For the end of the end. For no more time. For no more *mores* ...

He wishes his melancholy would take a *European* turn, Ede says, like Wittgenstein's.

EDE: Here, drink up! Maybe we can 'shroom our way to the fundament ...

A walk on the Backs.

Thought is also about knowing where to stop, Wittgenstein says. Sometimes, the thinker must desist from asking, *Why?* Sometimes, the thinker must let thought rest in peace.

His brother spoke of peace when he set off for Norway, Wittgenstein says. When he embarked for Norway, his brother hoped he would *solve every problem in philosophy*.

Norway would be his trial, his brother said, on the eve of his departure. Norway would be where he'd see if he was worthy of being called a thinker. Norway was where thought would writhe inside him, his brother said. *Through* him. Norway was where thought would flash above him, like the northern lights.

Norway was where he'd think his *severest* thoughts, his brother said. The most *terrible* of thoughts. Where thought would hurl its spear into him. Where thought, merciless, would *run him through*.

Norway would be too cold to let philosophy survive, his brother said. To let *what we know as philosophy* survive. The frozen air of Norway would kill all *philosophical germs*. Norway was death, his brother said. A certain *kind* of death.

By summer, he'd have solved all the fundamental problems of logic, his brother said. He'd have burrowed through the autumn, the winter, the spring. He'd have burrowed all the way to the Norwegian summer, to the never-ending day, when everything would be clear.

The truth, at first, would be unbearable, his brother said.

Hard to get used to. Hard to *endure*. Because truth was also a judgement. Because truth would judge you, and find you wanting.

The truth would know his sins, his brother said. The truth would expose all his darknesses.

There would be no secrets in the Norwegian summer, his brother said. Nothing would be hidden. The truth would know him. God would know him, in the summer light.

The truth would search him, his brother said. It would search through him. He'd breathe the truth down to the bottom of his lungs. He'd inhale and exhale the truth.

His soul would be *light*, his brother said. His soul would *weigh nothing*. He would feel his soul rising in the Norwegian summer. His soul would float into the air like a fire-balloon.

And there would be silence, his brother said. There would be nothing he *needed* to say.

He'd barely sleep, his brother said. There would be no need for sleep in the never-ending day. There would be no need to rest. No need to dream under the never-setting sun.

The stars would dream, above the sky. The planets would dream for him, as they fell through the darkness.

His heart would be bright, his brother said. His heart would pulse like a jellyfish in the sunlit waters. And pale stars would show in the upper heavens. And God's angels would be there, just above the sky. And God's throne would stand in the middle of the sky. And God's face would no longer be hidden. And God would be everywhere, just as light would be everywhere. There would be no corner of darkness where the devil might hide.

In the shadowless summer, he'd live in innocence, his brother said. In lightness. In grace. And his soul would be as transparent as the wings of summer insects. And he would think as birds flit from branch to branch. As fish nuzzle the surface of the water. The thought of life would be indistinguishable from life. Thought would live. Life would think ...

When his brother returned from Norway, Wittgenstein went to meet him at the airport, he says. He saw his brother, as he walked through arrivals, his rucksack on his back. His brother was thinner. There was more grey in his hair. Ice-flecks. And there was more *depth* in his eyes. A touch of *horror*, though his eyes were still kind and bright.

That night, over dinner, his brother spoke of the black depths of the fjord, and of the mountains which come all the way down to the water's edge. He spoke of wooden houses and forests of conifer. He spoke of the dim light of autumn afternoons; of days fading, having never really begun; and of the frozen suspense of winter—of the sparkle of hoar-frost and of thick banks of snow.

To be in Norway was to be back at the beginning of the world, his brother said. The great ice-hewn rocks were as though left over from the creation. The pack ice in the fjord was like chunks of light. The mountain rivers were as pure as ice ...

His brother spoke of Norwegian *tears*, frozen on his cheeks. He spoke of Norwegian *laughter*, bursting out in the crystalline air. He spoke of Norwegian *joy*, rising like sap in the conifers.

He'd feared only the *Norwegian storms*, his brother said. When the sky seemed to be tearing itself apart. To be tearing *him* apart. The storms of Norway: he'd have wished them on no one. They'd exhausted him. He'd lost days of work. How many times had he taken to his bed like an invalid, ringing down to the village for supplies?

But there was joy in recovering his strength after these storms, his brother said. There was joy in convalescing, as after a terrible illness. As after a fit of madness. In the silence of his cabin, he had felt his strength trickling back. Listening to the icicles drip-drip-drip, he had known himself to be coming to life again. And one day, he'd forced his water-swollen door open, and laughed as moisture clouded from his mouth.

There were *Norwegian despairs*, deeper and truer than his English despairs, his brother said. He'd feared their *depths*. But he'd been *awed* by them, too. His despairs had been as impersonal as the Norwegian landscape.

Oxford despair had always made him feel flat and sluggish, his brother said. Oxford turns you vague. Diffuse. Your soul *dissipates* in an Oxford despair. It dissolves as into a mist. But a Norwegian despair gathers you together, his brother said. Norwegian despair makes you coalesce. Consolidate. Norwegian despair places you—*you*—on trial. It summons *you*, just you, for judgement.

It's as though the stars fling down their spears at you, his brother said. As though the stars burn in your flesh. Quite terrible! How alone you become! How cut-off! But how *pure* you become, too. There is no one around you. You are lonely. But it's as though your loneliness is cauterised. As though your wounds glow with light. As though they are touched by frost-fire.

He'd dreamt of making a *logical expedition* to the northernmost reaches of Norway, across the ice field, his brother said. He'd dreamt of venturing forth, across the great glacier, striding over crevasses, with a notebook in his pocket. He'd dreamt of heading where no sane man would ever go.

He'd dreamt of making preparations for setting off. Of learning to breathe at high altitude. Of taking deeper and deeper breaths. Of acclimatising himself to the far north and to the farther north.

And he'd dreamt of heading forth one crisp, clear morning. Of setting off, before anyone had woken, as dawn broke. Of climbing up and up and up, following the course of the river to the foot of the glacier, and then climbing onto the ice. And then walking forth across the ice, up and only up, the sunlight dazzling his eyes.

He'd dreamt of the cairn left to commemorate his ascent. Of the legends that would remain of his disappearance. And he'd dreamt of his own dead body, somewhere high and far and sun-touched. He'd dreamt of his frozen body, there above the clouds, there in the element of truth. There, where the winter sun blazed. There, where everything was frost-fire sharp and ice-clear.

And he'd dreamt of his frozen notebooks, full of truth, his brother said. He'd dreamt of his indecipherable writing, full of truth. He'd dreamt of the path he had trailed that none could follow. He'd dreamt that he had *died* of truth, of terrible truth. That truth had thrown its spear through him. That truth's tears had frozen on his cheeks.

The highest idea. The loneliest idea. How clearly it shined, for those who could see it! How absolute, broken from everything, for those who knew where to look! An idea like a star, a white star, blazing coolly. An idea broken off and burning by itself, exulting in darkness by itself.

Would he have reached it, that star, with his death? Would death have been the way that sun reached to him and touched him? Would his death have been the touch of that sun, the touch of *truth*?

. . .

Spring came, his brother said. The days grew longer. He hadn't been able to sleep. It was too bright. The light was merciless.

He'd felt like the *last* philosopher. The *only* philosopher, living on until he could bring philosophy to an end. Endless consciousness … Endless vigilance … Awake, awake, awake until the end of time. Was that to have been his sentence, until he'd brought philosophy to rest?

He'd been awake as no one had been awake before him, his brother said. He'd been awake for everyone, for all the insomniacs whose heads burn like lanterns beneath the starry night.

The mind meditating on the mind. The brain thinking constantly of itself. Thinking about thinking. Thinking about thinking about thinking. When would it stop?, his brother had asked himself.

His brother had sought calm, Wittgenstein says. He'd sought order. He'd sought to stand like God over the elements, before the creation. *Let there be order*, he'd wanted to say. *Let there be goodness.*

His brother had sought, in his logic, to create a sanctuary on the face of the abyss. His brother had sought to uphold all particularities and inherent distinctions. He'd sought to safeguard the *measure* of the Creation, the divine Word that keeps everything in its place.

His brother had sought to hold back the waters of the Deep and the monsters of the Deep. He'd sought to preserve the structure of speech. He'd sought to renew the grammar of language, to strengthen its syntax. To keep hold of the names of things, along with the relations between them.

But logic wouldn't obey his brother. Chaos came. The paths were drowned. The Creation was breached. A sea of evil flooded the world. And the fixed order of things was swept away ...

Unformed thoughts; void thoughts: that's what Wittgenstein's brother wrote about in his final notebook. He wrote of storms of meaninglessness; of pure, brute being. Of regions in which even the law of non-contradiction fails, in which nothing is identifiable. In which the non-Word devours the Word ...

His brother wrote of *nothingness* in his final notebook. Of nihilism adrift, spreading everywhere. He wrote of meaninglessness alive. Of the eleven dimensions of the void unfolding ... He wrote of *collapse*—inward *and* outward. He wrote of *hollowness*. Of *implosion*. Of the erosion of the soul.

His brother wrote of the *logical pandemonium* in his final notebook. Of the *logical calamity*. He wrote of the *shipwreck* of logic. He wrote of extinguished stars. Of ghost galaxies, long burnt out. He wrote of dark matter. Dark energy. He wrote of the end of the world, and of the endless end of the world. He wrote of *living* death and *dying* life ...

Cindie's. Saturday night. A dance-off between Mulberry and Doyle. Criteria: flair, originality, acrobatics.

Doyle comes on, high-fiving his audience before ambitiously referencing the entire history of dance. Witch-doctor trance. Warriors' huddle. Doyle *en pointe*, holding his pose. Doyle in the ballroom, sweeping round the floor. A burst of tap. The *Charleston. Swing.* Then the *Lindy Hop.* And, from left field, Brazilian *capoeira* ...

Chakrabarti sees some Indian classical moves in Doyle's repertoire; Okulu, some Nigerian Alanta. Doyle locks and pops, waves and vogues and robots. Then, a scissor leap, before a final John Travolta.

A *postmodern* performance, we decide. Eclecticism! Hybridism! Everything at once! Refreshing—but also *innovating*. Alexander Kirwin gives it a nine; Benedict Kirwin, an eight; Titmuss, a seven. Total: twenty-four.

Mulberry's turn. He freezes for a full minute, as if in bullet-time. Then the full *moonwalk*, up and down the floor, white towelling socks gleaming. Then, *comedy*—Mulberry claws his hands and pretends to crawl across the dance floor as up a mountain slope; Mulberry catches a hooked finger in his mouth, hauling himself towards the DJ, like a fish struggling on the line. Then, *tragedy*—Mulberry pulls a toreador's cloak over his narrow frame, and dances *flamenco*, full of *duende*. Then he slows down, holding poses, with the hyper-control of *Butoh.* Mulberry is Agony, Mulberry is Suffering. Mulberry is Hurt, Mulberry is Dying, Mulberry is Death ...

Mulberry dances the *End of Dance*. Then Mulberry dances the *Posthumous Dance*.

What pathos! What emotion! Innocence lost. Perhaps innocence destroyed! Alexander Kirwin gives it an eight, Benedict Kirwin gives it an eight, Titmuss gives it an eight. Total: twenty-four—a dead heat. The dance-off must go to a dance-off.

Tension: Mulberry and Doyle facing each other, each daring the other to begin—two slim sumo wrestlers, half squatting, hands on thighs.

Release: the *paso doble*, Mulberry as the matador, and Doyle, by turns, the matador's cape, the matador's shadow, the bull itself; the *Carimbó*, Doyle spinning Mulberry like a top and then, old-style, in three-quarter time, in tiny, delicate steps, Mulberry leading; then, *grinding*, doggy-style, Doyle behind Mulberry, Mulberry behind Doyle; then the closing scene of *Dirty Dancing*, as if they rehearsed it for weeks, Mulberry/Johnny holding an outstretched Doyle/Baby above his head. What a climax! What a resolution!

The judges are overjoyed. Alexander Kirwin: ten! Benedict Kirwin: ten! Titmuss: ten! Mulberry and Doyle lead everyone in a conga, snaking from the dance floor out onto the streets ...

In the weeks after his brother's suicide, Wittgenstein read his brother's notebooks in his Cambridge rooms.

Sometimes, he opened the notebooks reverently, as though they were the holiest of texts. He followed the strict sequence of proofs in his brother's meticulous handwriting. He marvelled at the boldness of his brother's formulae, his new logical language. At the new logical operators his brother used.

At other times, he opened the notebooks at random, alighting on this proof, or on that, or puzzling over one of his brother's occasional remarks. (*Truth is indivisible, hence it cannot recognise itself. The only way to truth is through one's own annihilation. Torment is the beginning of religion. The will to think is the will to pray ...*)

He slept with his brother's notebooks beside him on his bed, Wittgenstein says. He had confused dreams, logical dreams, of drawing his brother's reflections into a systematic unity. Of organising his brother's writings into a complete and definitive form.

His brother's notebooks were eccentric, Wittgenstein says. Some might say *mad*. The calm handwriting of the first notebook (tiny, neat, controlled, upright) gave way to the wilder handwriting of the second notebook (larger, florid, looped, forwards-leaning), and to the deranged handwriting of the third notebook (words obscure, often indecipherable, written as though in a kind of code, as though his brother wanted to *hide* what he wrote, as though he wanted to *conceal* it, even from himself).

Carefully numbered points, an architectonic structure for his logical project, gave way to scraps, fragments. To shifting sands. Meticulous proofs, scrupulous formulae, gave way to remarks *about* his project. About the *impossibility* of his project. About the impossibility of *logic*. About the impossibility of *philosophy*.

There were times when he deliberately *neglected* his brother's notebooks, Wittgenstein says. Their demand was too great. Their challenge, too frightening. He rested mugs of coffee on their covers. He left them at the bottom of his rucksack, squashed by supermarket groceries, pastry grease staining their pages.

There were times when he wanted to *off-load* his brother's notebooks, Wittgenstein says. To have done with his responsibilities. He thought of placing them in a Jiffy bag and posting them anonymously to the Bodleian. He thought of leaving them on the doorstep of the British Library. He thought of sending the notebooks to the Oxford philosophy department. To Cambridge lecturers in logic. But who would understand them?

Only one who has had exactly the same thoughts that I have had can understand me, his brother wrote in his first notebook. *Only one who has suffered thought, who has suffered his way to thought. Only one, like me, who went to logic on his hands and knees.*

I have come to Norway to suffer for logic, and perhaps die for logic, or at the very least go mad for logic, his brother wrote in his second notebook. *Logic will no doubt send me mad. But it will be a sublime madness. A sane madness.*

Clarity or death. No—clarity is death, his brother wrote in his third notebook. *I am dead. I am no longer human. Only the dead can read these pages.*

News! Professor Warrington-Smythe, head of philosophy at Oxford, is coming to give a paper. Will Wittgenstein attend, we wonder, to face down the famous philosopher?

The ancient debating chamber, on the main campus. Warrington-Smythe, with a group of Oxford students. And the big guns of Cambridge: Professor Crookshank, Ellison Chair in Logic, with a band of *his* students. Professor Knowles, McCarthy Chair in Political Philosophy, with a band of *his* students ... Are all of the Cambridge philosophers here?

Bell, in sandals, whispering in James's ear. Powell, all tweed, giggling with Harding. Raynor-Scobey, eyes closed as she listens. Twelvetrees, furiously taking notes. Clutterbuck, folding an origami swan. Turner-Whitford, his chair tilted back, feet resting on the desk in front of him. Scotswood, clicking his pen, looking fierce, ready for battle ...

Wittgenstein, unobtrusive in his beltless mackintosh, seated by a window at the back of the room. What has brought him here, we wonder, he who loathes all Cambridge philosophy, and, we suppose, all Oxford philosophy? Why has he come, who doesn't believe in *Oxbridge philosophy*?

Warrington-Smythe blows his nose and coughs loudly. His students also cough, and also blow *their* noses. Crookshank rubs his bald head back and forth with both hands. Crookshank's students rub their thick hair back and forth with both hands, making a curiously leonine effect. Knowles surreptitiously fingers his nostrils. Knowles's students surreptitiously finger *their* nostrils.

Wittgenstein, meanwhile, looks out of the window. And we, too, look out of the window.

Afterwards, Ede's rooms.

EDE: That was unbearable. Warrington-Smythe was awful!

DOYLE: Crookshank was just as bad. Actually, Crookshank was *worse*!

MULBERRY: Did you hear bloody Knowles? He does go on.

DOYLE: Who do you think won, Oxford or Cambridge?

MULBERRY: They were both bloody awful.

But what of Wittgenstein's silence?, we wonder. Was it a form of *instruction*? Ought we somehow to learn from it?

Perhaps Wittgenstein's just *sad*, I speculate. Perhaps he's simply lost in despair.

Doyle remembers Wittgenstein's face as cracked in woe. But Mulberry says Wittgenstein's face was expressionless. It betrayed nothing.

His silence was like a black hole, we agree. A void in the conference. As though he sucked the occasion into himself, making it nothing. We were uneasy. What did Wittgenstein want of us, in the aftermath of Oxbridge philosophy?

We fantasise that Wittgenstein had *wiped the floor* with Crookshank and his Oxford contingent. That he had raised his hand at the end of Crookshank's paper. *With respect...*, he had begun, obviously meaning the *complete opposite*. *I would like to make a few modest remarks ...* , he had continued, all but pulling on a knuckleduster.

That Wittgenstein had blinded everyone! Left them dazzled. That Oxford had been ashamed, that Cambridge had been ashamed. That *Oxbridge* had been shown to itself in all its corruption. That *Oxbridge philosophy* had learnt its lesson.

That all had known a giant sat amongst them. That the very presence of Wittgenstein had been a living reproach. That Wittgenstein had humbled Oxford, and brought Cambridge to its knees.

That it hadn't been about point scoring—about petty academic politics. That it had been about the essential nobility of thought ... the pure spirit of inquiry ... of philosophy! About Wittgenstein's essential *incorruptibility* ...

That the whole of *Oxbridge* had marvelled. That all there had wondered at us, Wittgenstein's pupils. That we had shone with some of Wittgenstein's majesty.

But Wittgenstein has told us many times that philosophy *has nothing at all to do with discussion*; that philosophy *eschews* debate; that one should *do* philosophy, and not *talk* philosophy.

Wittgenstein headed up his stairwell, alone and quite silent, only nodding at us to take his leave. We heard the sound of his brogues on the flagstones. He seemed weary. His steps slowed. Had he reached the top of the staircase? Was he unlocking the door of his rooms?

What *might* he have done?, we wonder. Might he have stood, at some point, and said some splendid, gnomic thing, something no one had understood, not even us? Some splendid, gnomic thing that had stunned everyone, that had given them pause, that had *halted the whole charade*, if only for a moment. Some splendid thing, impenetrable, gnomic, at once absolutely relevant and absolutely baffling.

Might he have left, pulling on his mackintosh? And might we have followed, Wittgenstein's men, glamour and mystery trailing after us, myth and legend already beginning to accrete around us? Might the legend of Wittgenstein have really begun? The legend of Wittgenstein and his men. Of a new thought-prince, and a new thought-school. Of a new step in philosophy, a strange step, a knight's move, to leap over the heads of current thinkers. A new zigzag, a bolt of thought striking down, leaving nothing intact. Might Wittgenstein have left the ancient hall, mackintosh billowing? Might we have left with him, mackintoshes billowing?

We'd hoped for more, we admit. Not just from Wittgenstein, but from everyone. We'd hoped for better things of academic debate.

We'd imagined battles of logic, played out on parallel whiteboards, formulae flying from logician's fingers.

We'd imagined the to-and-fro of medieval disputations. Like chess games. Like speed chess, the moves coming faster and faster. Until the loser gasped for air, exhausted, and the winner sat back in triumph.

We'd imagined rival casuists, rival applied ethicists, at war over the interpretation of particular cases. (The plank of Carneades. Foot's *trolley problem*. Parfitt's *mere addition* paradox.)

We'd imagined philosopher-exegetes, competing to give the best gloss of Gödel's *Formally Undecidable Propositions*. Of Tarski's *Concept of Truth*. Of Łukasiewicz's *Elements of Mathematical Logic*.

We'd dreamt of old thinkers, charging around the philosophical landscape like tyrannosaurs, before being brought down by the fiendish cunning of a pack of young velociraptors. We'd dreamt of old thought-warriors crashing to the ground, the referee counting slowly to ten.

We'd imagined tag teams of Cambridge thinkers: the metaphysician teamed with the philosopher of mind; the logician teamed with the Kant-specialist ...

We'd imagined thought-wars: *quietists* against *stridentists*, *cognitivists* against *non-cognitivists*, *moral particularists* against *moral absolutists*, *physicalists* against *dualists* ...

We'd imagined secret thought-battles, for philosophers only, clandestine after-conferences like the after-show catwalk battles in *Zoolander* ...

Yes, we had hoped for more, we agree.

He knows what philosophy is, Wittgenstein says. He has seen the face of philosophy. He has seen the face of logic.

The look of *torment* on his brother's face. The look of *calamity* on his brother's face. The look of *despair* on his brother's face. He has seen these things.

The look of *relief* on his brother's face, when they cut down his body. The look of *peace* on his brother's face, when they closed his eyes. Of *achieved* peace, as at the end of a late Beethoven quartet. Yes, he has seen these things, he says.

Philosophy invaded his brother, Wittgenstein says. It saw a chink, a weakness, and flooded in.

There never was any such thing as logic, his brother wrote in his first notebook. *The whole of the history of logic is only an episode in the history of the impossibility of logic.*

There never was any such thing as philosophy, his brother wrote in his second notebook. *The history of philosophy is only a chapter in the greater history of madness.*

Logic is mad, his brother wrote in his third and final notebook. *All reason is mad. Thought has gone mad, lost in its corridors. Thought has sent itself mad, thinking about itself in its labyrinth.*

His brother wrote of thoughts of infinite recursion, of mirrored mirrors. He wrote of thoughts of the abyss that are themselves an abyss. He wrote of thoughts of darkness that are themselves dark. He wrote of thoughts of the end that never *reach* the end.

There is another, thinking inside me, his brother wrote in his final notebook. *There is another, unthinking my thoughts. Unliving my life. Another, dying my life and living my death ...*

Philosophy: the name for the disaster of thought, his brother wrote in his final notebook. *Philosopher: the name for the other, who thinks inside me.*

Then it came to him, Wittgenstein says: his task, the task he would take on for his brother's sake, and in his brother's memory. He would construct a kind of *logical mausoleum* for his brother. What is his *Logik* but a logical *tomb* for his brother? And the logical *resurrection* of his brother?

He means to enter the region in which his brother lost his mind, and to come back out, Wittgenstein says.

A first snowfall. Winter already!

Ede and I, on the way to class, contemplating the transitoriness of life.

How much time do we have left? How many days until the end of term? Until the end of the academic year? We long for it all to be over. We *dread* that it will all be over.

A burning desire to bunk off. To hit the road in Ede's coupé.

How *open* our lives are, just as Wittgenstein says! Anything might happen! We are lost. Lost in the middle of life. We feel vulnerable—alone and exposed, falling deeper and deeper into Time.

We may have sniffed too much amyl nitrate last night, Ede says. He thought his head would *burst*. And there were too many Black Zombies ...

But it's more than that, we agree. We've begun to *think* about our lives. To think about our *thoughts*! To ask ourselves who we are, and what made us who we are. And our questions resound inside us: Why is there anything at all? Why is there life? Why death? Whose gift was all this? Whose mistake was it all? Whose *boon*? Whose oversight? By what law of necessity did it occur? By what blind chance? What's it all for? Why should it be *for* anything?

Wittgenstein would approve, Ede says. We're acquiring *depth* ...

. . .

Chakrabarti, walking ahead of us, babbling to Wittgenstein. Of all people! For fuck's sake!

Chakrabarti wears a padded coat, all the way down to his feet, like a duvet ... And his *grin*. His goonish grin ...

What's Chakrabarti *doing* in Cambridge anyway? What's he doing in our class? Why's he always padding after us like the fat kid in Hollywood movies? Why, when he has no chance whatsoever of understanding Wittgenstein?

Chakrabarti is out of his depth, we agree. Chakrabarti should have kept to the shallows, splashing about. Chakrabarti should have stayed on the beach, playing with his sand castles.

Chakrabarti signed up for the *Cambridge experience*—that we're sure of. Chakrabarti, in the Cambridge sweatshirt, now and forever a *Cambridge man*.

Chakrabarti lacks any sense of irony ... Chakrabarti is without depth, which surprises us—India is *the* country of spiritual depth! What happened, we wonder? What went so wrong over there, that India could produce a Chakrabarti?

Chakrabarti, grinning back at us. How inane he is! But we have to admit that Chakrabarti makes us feel clever, simply by comparison. Part of an elite. He makes us feel closer to Wittgenstein, in some way. *Akin* to him.

Growing pressure, growing urgency—Wittgenstein appears to believe that everything will soon fall into place.

He speaks quickly, *intimately*, presuming we can follow him.

Fewer pauses to think; fewer moments of silence. A pell-mell of logical symbols, of logical operators, of unfamiliar words. The blackboard on the mantle shelf written over and wiped clean.

Philosophy is simmering. Logic is being brought to the boil. Thought itself will soon be running over . . .

The last step is the hardest step, he says. The last step is the most *dangerous*. The last step requires the greatest courage. It is the step that changes the one who steps.

The end is not like the beginning, he says. The last hours are nothing like the first. Tomorrow is not another day.

He is carrying us with him, he says. Carrying us over the edge of thought's waterfall. We will tumble into thought's plunge pool together.

He means to whip up a logical storm, Wittgenstein says. A logical *frenzy*. He means to shake the snow globe of logic. He means to send it mad. And he means to *welcome* madness when it comes. He means to let it destroy him. He means to let it destroy the world—what he *knows* as the world.

The resurrection of *thought*. That's what he means to find. The resurrection of the *world*.

He means to drown everything in the baptismal bath of his *Logik*, Wittgenstein says. He will baptise everything anew—when the *Logik* is revealed, we, too, will be revealed. We will know who we are. No: we will *be* who we are. At the end, the very end, we will *put on* the *Logik*, Wittgenstein says. We will wear the *Logik* as an *armour of light* …

A walk on the Backs.

The *don-watch*, that's what he calls his late-night vigils, Wittgenstein says. When he can't sleep, he sits by the window, he says, and peers out into the gloom. There are dons out there, he tells himself. Hundreds of them. Thousands of them! There are dons in the gloom, near and far. Flocks of dons! *Shoals* of dons! Where one banks, the others bank. Where one careens, the others careen. Sometimes, they all fly up at once— a comet, a maelstrom, a boiling mass—and their wings hide the skies …

Yes, there is a real splendour to dons *en regalia*, he says. A real beauty to dons in their full plumage. The dons, with their chests puffed out … The dons, with their erect carriage … The dons, in their hierarchies, which are intelligible to no one … The dons, carrying out their ceremonial duties, which not even they understand …

The dons have a kind of *pack* intelligence, he says. A *hive* intelligence; they think in unison. Sometimes, he's even suspected that the dons are *telepathically connected*, so similar do they seem to him in manner and in thought.

The dons are always ready to pounce, he says. Always ready with their greetings. *Hello*, they say. *Nice weather we're having,* they say. *How are you?*, they say. *How are you getting on?*, they say. *What have you been up to?*, they say. Each time: an assault. Each time: a truncheon over the head. *Hello. Nice day. Hello. Hello.*

And the philosopher-dons are worst of all!, he cries.

The dons of ethics—the least *virtuous* of all. The dons of logic—the least *reasonable* of all. The dons of epistemology—the least *knowledgeable* of all. The dons of metaphysics—the least *profound* of all. The dons of aesthetics—the least *cultured* of all ...

The dons of philosophy: academic-output manufacturers! Impact-seekers! Grant-chasers! Citation-trufflers! Self-googlers! Web-profile updaters! Facebook posters! Tweedy voids!

Do the dons know about his *Logik*?, he wonders. Have any of us told them?

No, we assure him. None of us has told them.

Do the dons know about him, about what he is teaching?

No, we tell him. We have kept our mouths shut.

What would the dons do if they knew?, he whispers.

The *Logik* will solve all the fundamental problems of philosophy, he says.

The *Logik* will soar above the philosophical storms. It will catch fire by itself. It will burn with its own flame, like a star.

The *Logik* will know everything, he says. It will have seen everything in advance. The *Logik* will be lucidity itself. Daylight itself.

The *Logik* will bring *peace*, he says. Logical peace.

Snow scenes, as in Brueghel. Students making snowmen. Students throwing snowballs at one another.

Benwell, in the thick of it, throwing snowballs packed with stones.

Ede and I, at a safe distance.

Why does Benwell scowl so?, we wonder. And what's it like to be in a *bad temper* day and night?

Benwell would throw his stone-balls at us, if we were in range. Benwell would curse and cry and spit at us ...

In the old days, Benwell would have been a communist, or something, we agree. He'd have been selling socialist papers in the rain, or getting you to sign a petition. He'd have been manning the *Free Palestine* stand. Even a few years ago, he'd have been among the occupiers in the Old Buildings, shuffling around in dirty pyjamas ...

Ede remembers field days on Chobham Common, he and his fellows forming up and crawling through the heather, re-enacting the great battles of history. Schoolboy-Agincourt. Schoolboy-Waterloo. The schoolboy *trenches*, boys going over the top into muddy no-man's-land.

You were supposed to take off your beret when you were 'shot', Ede says. Actually, you *hoped* to be shot, so you could pretend-die in slo-mo, and then sit and eat your sandwiches in the sun ...

And you'd trail toilet paper out the window on the train home. And form up again on the platform at Windsor station.

And be played back to school by the drums corps from Victoria Barracks ...

And all the while, Ede says, he'd dream of finding live weaponry and running amuck on Founder's Day. Of firing a Gatling gun from the school roof, and hurling mortars from the spiked gables ...

Perhaps, when he inherits it, he should turn his family estate into a terrorist training camp, Ede says. Declare war on the bourgeois world. He could form a new Weather Underground, a new Baader-Meinhof. He could kidnap bankers and blow up the stock exchange. Ede laughs.

He'll probably just turn it into an anarchist commune, Ede says. Grow vegetables on the west lawn. Fill the lake with trout. Live in teepees on the old veranda. And let the house itself fall into ruin. Or, he might just torch the whole thing, like Nero, and rock back and forth on his heels.

Benwell's too late for politics, and we are too late for politics, Ede says. Too late for the Occupation. Too late to march on the streets ...

Guthrie, lying in the snow, quite drunk. An involuntary snow angel. His lips are blue. There's frost in his wispy beard. He looks noble, we agree. Like some recently deceased Arctic explorer.

The rumour is that Guthrie drinks because of some great and secret tragedy. That Guthrie drinks in the *tragic mode*— that his drinking is a lament, a eulogy. That Guthrie is ruining his life because he doesn't want to live. That Guthrie drinks *deliberately*, knowing where it will lead. That Guthrie is looking for oblivion, because he's seen too much. Because he's been out farther than us all ...

EDE: Guthrie's a sot. But we're all sots! And at least Guthrie's got a greatness about him.

Ede kicks Guthrie. Nothing. He kicks him again.

Ede unscrews the cap of his hip flask under Guthrie's nose. Guthrie stirs.

EDE: Entertain us, Guthrie. Put on a show.

Guthrie's eyes, bloodshot, blank, looking up at us. Ede administers a pill to Guthrie's drool-caked mouth, and pours the contents of his hip flask after it.

We wait, stomping our feet to keep warm. Ede does star jumps. I do squat thrusts. Ede throws snowballs at me. I throw snowballs at Ede.

EDE (contemplating Guthrie): To think that he once performed Marcus Aurelius!

We recall Guthrie's finest hour, his portrayal of the emperor-philosopher.

Doyle's rooms, at the beginning of term. Salt. Lime. Tequila.

A martial scene: the Romans versus the Barbarians, along the shore of the Danube (Guthrie as the Roman army; Guthrie as the Barbarian horde; Guthrie as the wide river itself). Clouds of dust. The plain covered in carcasses. Groans of the dying (Guthrie groans). Broken spears. The ground slippery with blood. Heaps of the dead (Guthrie as a corpse; Guthrie as a pile of corpses). Lifeless corpses trampled on without mercy. The columns broken back (Guthrie as a broken army, staggering and moaning). The half-slain blocking up the roads ...

The imperial encampment: Marcus Aurelius, writing in his tent (Guthrie, all nobility, all gravitas). Marcus, tired of war, tired of a decade of campaigning (Guthrie, weary). Marcus, seeking to triumph over the passions and recognise the will of God in all events (Guthrie, a man of piety, a man of philosophy). Marcus, unwavering even in the midst of his duties (Guthrie, a man of resolve).

The battlefield: Marcus, surveying the scene (Guthrie, eyes on the middle distance). Marcus, speaking to his soul (Guthrie, speaking to his soul): *All that is in tune with you, O universe, is in tune with me.* Marcus, seeing the bodies of enemy soldiers twisted into impossible shapes (Guthrie, wincing): *We must love even those who commit injustices against us.* Marcus, seeing the dead faces of his own soldiers turned to the cold earth (Guthrie, shuddering): *Despise not death, but welcome it, for nature wills it like all else.* Marcus, seeing the blood of his soldiers on the frozen ground (Guthrie, crestfallen): *Tomorrow is nothing, today is too late, the good lived yesterday.*

Wittgenstein is weary. His face is grey.

He is exhausted, he says, not from doing anything. He is without *real life*.

If he were only capable of working, he says.

Why is the drive to understand so close to the drive to *mis*understand?, he asks. Why is the urge to think almost identical with the urge *not to think*?

Truth sends no news, he says, with unusual emphasis. (Is he quoting?)

Libera me, Domine, he says. (Definitely quoting.)

God is calling him, he says. God is hunting him down. He's fleeing God's call. It's all he's ever done: flee God's call.

To reach the end of thought, he says. To bring thought to an end. But at the end of thought, there is also the *thought* of the end. At the end of thought, there is also the *thought* of the end of thought ...

Any *real* thinker would go mad, he says. Any real thought is also a *mad* thought.

He holds his head in his hands. He shakes his head slowly.

What does God want from him?, he asks. What does God expect from him?

A shaft of winter light.

He stirs slightly. Has he found an answer? A solution?

A badly timed fit of laughter breaks out somewhere near Mulberry.

Ede (refined laughter). Then the Kirwins (synchronised laughter).

What was it? Mulberry's gigantic cock drawing (sketched for Doyle's amusement)? Doyle's knocking Titmuss's can of Red Bull into Benedict Kirwin's open sports bag, in a spasm of hilarity? The copy of *XXX Mums*, revealed when Benedict Kirwin leaned forward to retrieve the can? Chakrabarti's squeal when Alexander Kirwin thumped him on the leg to distract the class from *XXX Mums*? Okulu, stomping out of the room in indignation at the chaos?

Wittgenstein—looking baffled. Wittgenstein—looking frustrated. What's wrong with us? What are we laughing at? Has someone told a *joke*? Has someone done something *funny*? *He* has heard no joke, he says. *He* has heard nothing funny.

Has *he* said something funny?, he asks. Has *he* said something ridiculous? A faux pas? A double entendre? He knows how we English love our double entendres.

Our laughter dies away. Silence.

Wittgenstein—looking exhausted.

What can one man do alone?, he mutters.

Why do we come to his classes?, Wittgenstein asks us. Why, when philosophy is not of the least consequence to us? When we do not *need* philosophy? When we do not *suffer* from our need for philosophy?

What is it like not to have an idea in our heads? What is it like to *believe* in nothing, to be *engaged* by nothing, to *strive* for nothing, to *suffer* for nothing, to have nothing in particular for which to live or die? What's it like to feel *content*? To feel *pleased with ourselves*? What is it like to *smile at ourselves in the mirror*? What is it like to laugh without fear?

. . .

A *Punch and Judy* show—that's what he is, Wittgenstein says. Playing the fool for us. Jingling his cap and bells.

He's the clown brought in to amuse us. To keep us entertained. To keep us occupied before we begin the *real business of life*.

We smile—just like the dons. We indulge him, we *enjoy* him—just like the dons. But we tire of him, too—just like the dons. We are impatient with him, too—just like the dons. Perhaps laughing at him (a little). Perhaps with scorn (a little scorn). Smiling at him, but *tiring* of him, too. Smiling, smiling, but with a certain *impatience*.

Next!, we want to say—*we're tired of this one! Next!*, we demand—*bring us a fresh one!*

There's a fire backstage, he says. The clown comes out to warn the audience. Laughter and applause. They think it's a joke! The clown repeats his warning. The fire grows hotter; the applause grows louder. That's how the world will end, Wittgenstein says: to general applause, from halfwits who think it's a joke.

We should *hate* him, he says. We should *hate* thought, and the labour of thought. Because thought is opposed to everything we are. Logic is opposed to our very existence.

But we do not hate him, he says. We do not hate thought. Because there is a whole system to do the hating for us. A whole university—*Cambridge* University—that hates him and hates thought on our behalf.

We've *outsourced* our hatred, he says. We've sold it on, like a debt. We've subcontracted it, so that we can forget about it.

The university hates him in our place, he says. The dons hate thought, especially *his* thought, in our place.

WITTGENSTEIN: Cambridge hates me. Cambridge wants to destroy me. Well, Cambridge might have succeeded. *You* might have succeeded.

He slumps into a chair.

Silence.

Wie traurig!, he cries. What unhappiness!

Silence.

Mulberry in his *FUCK THE FUCK* T-shirt. Doyle, hand on Mulberry's arm. Titmuss, looking out of the window. The Kirwins, looking down at their trainers. Chakrabarti, looking up at the ceiling ...

The glass-fronted bookshelves, with their bound journals. A fly circling. The parquet floor. The humming computer. The cream-coloured radiators.

Silence.

Wittgenstein rises and leaves the room.

We wait, not knowing what to do.

Didn't he understand that our laughter didn't mean anything? That it was nothing personal? That it was least of all a judgement on him ...

Guilt. Should someone go after him?

Doyle walks out into the corridor, and back again.

No sign of him.

We file out, leaving the room empty behind us.

3

A walk on the Backs, without Wittgenstein.

Doyle, head sunk in guilt. Chakrabarti, shoulders hunched in shame. Mulberry, jacket pulled tight round his T-shirt, eyes lowered in repentance ...

With Wittgenstein we see ourselves as learners, as students, as eternal ephebes. We see ourselves as apprentices, as prodigies—as youths, eternal youths, on the brink of everything ...

We must admit it: we like the *romance of learning*. We like the romance of having *our very own thinker*. And who else but us will heed what he says?

The thinker is alone but for his pupils. The thinker rides the clouds in thought, stands on Atlas's shoulders, belongs to the starry heights—but only his pupils know it. The thinker is the open Delphi, looking upon visions beyond mortal sight—but only we, his students, can see it.

We have a duty to Wittgenstein. To witness. To record. To relay the Message. To watch over the gift of the Master ...

The next day. Ede and I at the porters' lodge. The usual bustle. *We're Wittgenstein's students. We want to ask him something.*

The porter makes a call.

Wittgenstein doesn't want to see anyone.

Ede and I tailgate two students past the porters' lodge, and climb the staircase to Wittgenstein's rooms.

We knock at his door. Silence. We bang at his door. Still silence.

We sit on the cold steps, waiting.

ME: You don't suppose anything's happened to him, do you? You don't think we've driven him to something? Remember what happened to his brother ...!

An hour passes. We salve our conscience by applying ourselves to the real Wittgenstein. Ede brings out the *Tractatus Logico-Philosophicus.* Tries to read it. Puts it away again. I pull out the *Philosophical Investigations.* Try to read it. Put it away again. Ede orders *Wittgenstein in 90 Minutes* on his phone.

We look up the Wittgenstein entry on Wikipedia. Very long! We search for pictures instead. A glum Wittgenstein, standing by a blackboard. A dour Wittgenstein, walking with a friend. Wittgenstein, gloomy in tartan. Wittgenstein, in profile—clearly suicidal.

We google *cheery Wittgenstein.* No results.

· · ·

We hear movement. From inside his rooms. The lock turns. The door opens. Wittgenstein, dishevelled but alive.

WITTGENSTEIN: What are you doing here?

EDE: We came to see if you were alright.

A pause.

WITTGENSTEIN (as from a great distance): I am not alright.

EDE: Look, we're very sorry we laughed. We didn't mean anything by it.

WITTGENSTEIN: You were right to laugh. (A pause.) How *dare* I teach a class! How dare I harm you by my teaching! (A longer pause.) All this talk of my *Logik*! Vainglory! Vanity!

Visible beyond the door: his table, a pile of notebooks, loose sheets, an open ledger—blank. Scraps of paper pinned to his walls, covered in handwritten proofs. In scrawled remarks. Just visible: *APERION*, in capital letters.

WITTGENSTEIN: There is no *Logik*! There's nothing, nothing. I am nothing. (Another long pause.) I heard laughter outside my room. Your laughter. I came out to hear you. I thought to myself, *There's a clue in their laughter. There's something I must find.*

His stare is very intense. *Desperately* intense, we agree afterwards.

Town. A concrete piazza, scattered with steel bollards. Surveillance cameras on high masts. New buildings, grotesquely aping the old ones, with decorative brickwork and painted gables. Office complexes with scholarly names (Academy House; Scholars' Grove, and so on).

WITTGENSTEIN: Cambridge has died, in its heart. It happened quickly. The rest of it will die much more slowly. (A pause.) A kind of rigor mortis has set in. A stiffness of the limbs. (A pause.) Cambridge is becoming *brittle*. Cracking, like ice in a puddle. Splintering. There are sharp edges in Cambridge. Careful! There are *spikes* and *shards*.

Near the station. Luxury apartments ('price on application') with stuck-on balconies. Investors' megaflats, with staring windows and slanted roofs on stilts.

He walks. We walk.

Thought is howling: can we hear it?, he says. *Logic* is howling. The wind is tearing the world to shreds. Now it begins: the great desolation. Now it will come: the storm of the cosmos.

The sky is cracking: can we hear it? The sky is about to shatter. The stars are stigmata drilling into the night. The earth is groaning. It sings, it groans.

• • •

Thought is exploding inside him, he says. Logic is exploding inside him.

Philosophy is loose inside him, he says. Philosophy is devouring him from within.

And when it has finished with him? When it has done devouring? But it will never finish with him, he says. There will always be more of him to destroy.

Belvedere Tower, domineering. The Leisure Park opposite—faceless, looming.

His brain is going out, he says. His brain is exploding.

He is being kept alive, he says. But for what purpose?

What does God want with him, by letting him live?

He has the sense of being *martyred*, but for no cause in particular.

He has the sense of being *bereft*, but without having lost anything in particular.

Homertown Street. Clone-town shops. Concrete and metal. Absolute blandness.

Thought, and the derangement of thought, he says. How to distinguish between them?

A break*down*, a break*through*: how to distinguish between them?

There is a *cost* to thought, he says. He'll pay with *himself*. He'll sacrifice *himself*.

. . .

Death, he says. He is drunk with death.

He can hear it: death is sharpening its knife. He can hear it: death is running its blade along the whetstone.

Death is coming, he says. Death will whistle around him like an Arctic storm.

Tea, among the tourists in the *Copper Kettle*.

Last night, he thought he saw the dons, looking up at his window and pointing, Wittgenstein says. He thought he heard the dons, shuffling up and down the stairs outside his room. He thought he sensed them, pacing back and forth on his landing. But when he looked out through his spyhole, there was no one there.

The dons are really pacing in his *head*, Wittgenstein says. The dons have set up court inside him. The dons are pronouncing judgement on him from the inside. A crowd of dons, jeering at him inside. *Sneering and jeering*: that's all he can hear inside his head, he says. There are hundreds, if not thousands, of dons, jostling inside him. A whole crowd of dons sneering inside him.

What do the dons want from him? What do they expect? What did they think he could bring to the university? What did they think he could contribute? Couldn't they see the kind of person he was? Wasn't it *clear*? He's never tried to hide what he is, Wittgenstein says. He's never pretended to be what he's not. His face—couldn't they read his face? Wasn't everything written there, on his face?

What did the dons think they'd found in him?, Wittgenstein asks. Who did they think they had brought to Cambridge? He was a curio, at first. A real find. Did they think he'd entertain them during the long winter nights? Because the dons need amusement, he says. The dons need diversion as the nights draw in.

But he has become too much for the dons, Wittgenstein says. He's become a *problem*, which the dons don't know how to solve. He is the equivalent of a blocked drain, he says. A blocked *lavatory*. What an unsavoury job to fix it! How will he be disposed of! It's not *my* job, each don says to himself. But then whose job is it?

It's *his* job, Wittgenstein says. *He* should dispose of *himself*. He should strangle himself, and get rid of the body. He should throw himself into the Cam, he says. He should throw himself off the *Mathematical Bridge*, or *Magdalene Bridge*, or *Cutter Ferry Bridge*, and let his body wash down to the sea.

It should be as though he had never been here, he says. As though he had never been invited to Cambridge, never brought here. The dons shouldn't be troubled by even the *memory* of his existence, he says. The dons shouldn't remember a thing—not a thing! The wound in their memory should be closed up ...

The dons should be left undisturbed, Wittgenstein says. The dons should be left to stride about on their English lawn. To walk with their hands behind their backs on the English lawn. To go in for English tea. To tuck into scones and jam in the English tea-room. The dons should be allowed to forget all about him. To never have heard his name. To have known nothing about him, about his very existence.

That his shadow has fallen on Cambridge: too much! That the shadow of Cambridge has fallen on him: too much! That his silhouette has been spied in the Cambridge evening: too much! That his feet have impressed the Cambridge turf ... That his breath has clouded the Cambridge morning ... That his eyes have rested upon Cambridge sights ... That his ears have been thronged with Cambridge noises ... Too much! too much! too much! too much!

Ah, but the dons know how it will end, he says. The dons can see the future. He will blow out his brains on the English lawn, they know that. And the lawnkeepers will rake out pieces of his skull from the English lawn.

We drive out to the country.

A clearing, ready for building. Stumps of trees. Diggers. Crates. Long metal pipes in piles. All for a new housing estate, beyond the suburbs of Cambridge.

A line of just-built houses without feature, blank-faced, simple. No shadows. No lines. A sheer wall of bricks and glass and plastic doors.

Red and blue *For Sale* signs. A show home on the corner. A flag by the show home, the developer's name flapping in the wind.

It may seem that Cambridge is expanding outwards, Wittgenstein says. That these are the new suburbs of Cambridge. But really it is the other way round. The suburbs are expanding *into* Cambridge. Cambridge is being engulfed by the suburbs. *Drowned* by them ...

What if he and his brother had lived ordinary lives?, Wittgenstein says. What if they had never embarked upon their *life of the mind*?

Why can he not accept the world as it is?, he says. Why is he unsatisfied with ordinary life? Why can he not let things be things, and the world be the world?

Plastic polytunnels. A wartime bunker with galvanised tin walls.

Sometimes, he wants only to *let it all go*, he says. To rest. To sleep. To let the world go its way. He dreams of a world that is liberated from him. Of a time when he is unremembered.

He dreams of his *disappearance*. Of the world without him. Of the world after his thought. After *all* thought. He dreams of having no need to think. He dreams of the light and grace of the world *after philosophy* …

He tells us a story.

Once upon a time, the devil made a mirror that mocked the things it reflected—that laughed at all beauty and goodness and grandeur. In his daring, the devil carried the mirror heavenward, so that he might use it to ridicule the angels, even to scorn the Saviour Himself. But, dazzled by heaven's light, the devil lost his grip as he flew upward. The mirror fell and shattered, and splinters of its mocking surface fell into the eyes and hearts of all human beings. And thereafter, all human eyes laughed at the Creation, and all human hearts laughed at love. And thereafter, there was no such thing as human innocence, nor human silence. And thereafter, there was no such thing as an innocent thought.

WITTGENSTEIN: That's how *philosophy* was born. Philosophy is a way of laughing at beauty and goodness and grandeur. A way of laughing at life!

EDE (gently): Then why do we bother with philosophy at all?

WITTGENSTEIN: Because philosophy stands between us and salvation.

Brightly coloured horse-jumps. A rider, circling the field, bobbing in the saddle.

Sometimes he wonders if we students aren't already on the other side of philosophy, he says. That philosophy, that all thought, is a matter for *him*, but not for *us*.

Are we the clue?, he asks. Are we the gateway out of philosophy? Perhaps the clue is in our faces. Perhaps it is there, right there. Perhaps the clue is in our laughter. If he could only *get to* our laughter …

A solitary horse in its field, standing by the fence. Wittgenstein leans forwards and breathes softly into its nostrils.

When he sees a horse, he feels that life itself is before him, he says. In truth, horses were never expelled from paradise. The horse, in particular, is close to the divine.

There was no better horseman than his father, Wittgenstein says. No better *man*!

He has no bad memories of his father—not one, he says.

WITTGENSTEIN: My father was a man of absolutes. Of *certainties*. (A pause.) A man of certainties can *act*. (A pause). My trouble is that I have no certainties, and therefore cannot act.

His mother was from a thinking family, Wittgenstein says. From a line of thinkers, from old Vienna. He had a thinking grandfather, he says. And a thinking grandmother. It goes back for generations.

They were Viennese Jews, his mother's family, he says. Then they were Viennese Catholics. Then, with the Anschluss, they were Viennese Jews again. *They haunt our steps, that we cannot go in our streets.* His great-grandfather paid off the Nazis, and the family fled the country, he says.

His mother was a *musical* thinker, he says. A concert pianist. She thought as she played. Reviewers wrote of her *fine equilibrium of intellect and emotion.* Of her *purity of style.* They wrote of her *polyphony.* Of her *unruffled perfection.* They wrote of the *morality* of her pianism. And of her *heart.*

It is possible to be *too good*, he says. My mother was *too good.*

Through the woods. Low beech branches close to the ground. Saplings in protective frames. Big, iron-coloured oaks.

You have to *want* to live, if you are to live, he says. That's what his brother lacked, he says: the desire to live.

We stop to make way for a Land Rover.

His brother showed *Lebenskraft*, he says—the *ability* to live. But his brother lacked *Lebenswille*—the *will* to live.

Sometimes, he, too, lacks *Lebenswille*, Wittgenstein says. But *we* are full of *Lebenswille*, he says, looking at us with affection. That is why he likes to keep us close.

A small brick outhouse. Then a barn, its doors open, giving into a greeny-black gloom.

The act of suicide means that anything is possible: that is its horror, he says. *Anything*: even striking against the grounds of life, the *life* of life.

Suicide *mocks* the possible, he says. It *laughs* at life. Death ought to come as *grace*, he says. As the gift of God. As even the *greatest* gift of God.

The end is not about the *will*, he says. We must not *want* the end. The end must come to us. The end must come, like a horse nuzzling our pockets for a treat.

What is divine is the fact that there is an end to our suffering, he says. That our end is coming.

The end is *innocent*, he says. It has God's innocence.

A canal lock. The black-and-white arms of the sluices. The lockkeeper's house, flying the flag of St George.

Thought was once a matter of *character*, Wittgenstein says. Of *living* in a certain way. You were judged as a thinker by the way you lived before others. You *showed* what you thought by the evidence of your life.

But thought, now, is a kind of *beetling*, he says. The thinker is a nocturnal insect. The thinker goes about in darkness. The thinker lives and dies unnoticed. His body is swept away with all the others, like a dried-up fly in a dusty corner.

Thinking is no longer an honest pursuit, he says. No longer a *decent* pursuit. There is something *covert* about thinking now. Something *dirty*.

The Fens. Open land, flat to infinity.

He doesn't like open spaces, Wittgenstein says. Before the sky, you can have no secrets. The light goes right through you. It leaves you no hiding place.

The sky is burrowing into him, he says. Why should he fear it?—the sky is blind; it sees nothing. But he feels that its blindness is itself an eye. An eye that *sees*. A blind eye—an eye that belongs to no one, that *sees*.

And it's not only the sky, he says. The earth watches

us, blindly. The toad that crawls through the clods of earth watches us, blindly. The circling rooks ...

Nothing is watching, he says. Nothingness *itself* is watching. He smiles. Imagine what his colleagues in Cambridge would think were he to speak to them of *nothingness itself*!

Life *cannot* go on as it is, he says. He has to die. He *must* die.

His mental suffering must be matched by a commensurate *physical* suffering, he says. He *must be* dying. He *must be* mortally ill.

How much time is left to him? A couple of months, he thinks. A couple of weeks.

Anything could happen, this close to the end, he says. The old laws do not apply anymore. At any moment, a slow tsunami could break over the Fens ...

Does water still swirl round the plughole in the same direction?, he wonders. Does the law of gravity still apply? Do compass needles still point north? Does one plus one still equal two? Does the moon still orbit the earth, and the earth, the sun?

Do the laws of physics still hold?, he wonders. If he walked in front of a bus, would it crush him? If he stabbed himself in the heart, would his heart stop beating? If he cut through his carotid artery, would he bleed to death? If he jumped from St Mary's, would his body splatter on the ground? If he drank a glass of cyanide, would he die of its toxicity?

He has a fear of time, Wittgenstein says. Of *open* time. Of empty moments. Empty hours. A fear of *intervals*. Of time that is not dedicated to a particular task. Time of which he is not the master. A fear of the thoughts that run through his head. Of the thoughts *about* thought that run through his head …

Life is too long, not too short, he says. Life is eternal.

He has experienced *every kind of mental illness*, he says. Not one mode of madness is closed to him. He's heard hostile voices. He's felt that his mind is being read. He's felt persecuted. Tormented, by alien forces. He's experienced great highs, manias. He's felt grandiosity. He's felt chosen. He's felt that only *he* could save the world.

And he's experienced terrible despairs, he says. Abysmal depression. He's had to keep away from sharp knives. From exposed pipework. From bottles of bleach. From high places …

He's hallucinated, he says. He's seen the skull of Cantor, full of worms. He's seen the brain of Gödel, invaded by maggots.

He's pulled out his hair. He's picked at his skin. He's counted his footsteps in intervals of two. He's sat, mute, for weeks on end, staring at the wall.

Has he ever known joy?, Wittgenstein wonders. Has he ever known happiness? Has he *lived*? Has he for one minute known what it means *to live*?

Has he ever *breathed*? Has he ever drawn a single breath? To breathe, to really breathe, must *hurt*—he's sure of it. To really breathe must give you *pain* in your lungs—at the bottom of your lungs.

Has he ever *looked*? Has he ever even *opened his eyes*? Has he ever *spoken*? Has he ever uttered anything *true*?

No one can speak the truth if he has not mastered himself, he says.

The truth can be spoken only by someone who is *at home* in the truth.

Everything must come from the heart, he says.

He wants to say only what he *has* to say. He wants to drop everything but the essential.

But what is it: the essential? What is it that he *has* to say?

Driving home through the Fens.

Flooded pasture. Meadows full of standing water. Saltwater wetlands. Tidal creeks and meres. Rivers braiding, fanning out.

You get a sense of what the Fens used to be like, before they were drained, Wittgenstein says. Settlers building on banks of silt, on low hills, on fen edges. Towns like islands in the marshland.

We imagine the first scholars, expelled from Oxford, founding the new university in Cambridge. We imagine the first colleges growing out of boardinghouses. The first classes, teaching priests to glorify God, and to preach against heresy. The first benefactors, donating money for building projects. The first courtyard design, at Queens College, the chapel at its heart. The first libraries, built above the ground floor to avoid the floods. The lands, drained along the river, and planted with weeping willows and avenues of lime trees. The Backs, cleared, landscaped lawns replacing garden plots and marshland. Cambridge, raising itself above the water. Cambridge, lifting itself into the heavens of thought ...

The rabbis thought that the old earth, Adam's earth, was as flat as the Fens, Wittgenstein says. That it enjoyed a perfect climate, a perfect summer. No extremes of weather—no thunder or ice, no snow or hail. It was the Flood that changed it all, the rabbis thought. It was the Flood that altered the surface of the earth.

Noah's ark came to rest on Ararat, Wittgenstein says. On the mountains. And Noah's family, and all their animals, had to go down from the mountains into the new valleys, into the changeable weather of the world.

His brother used to say that thought is always of the heights, Wittgenstein says. Of the mountains. The thinker must soar above everything. Close to the truth. Close to eternal things.

His brother dreamt of a *celestial* logic, Wittgenstein says. A system of logic that blazed in the sky. A logical system at one with the order of things, that might be divined in the order of things. A logic that God Himself must have studied, before embarking on the Creation.

It is a terrible thing for the thinker to be sent down from the heights, his brother told him—to be forced to return to the world.

But what if thought is *low*, and not high?, Wittgenstein says. What if the thinker's place is *below* things, or *with* things, rather than *above it all*?

What if to think is to *sink*, not to rise?, Wittgenstein says. What if thinking is falling, failing, defeat? What if thought is the *eclipse*, not the sun? What if thought is *mist*, not clarity? What if thought is getting lost, not discovering? What if thought is waylessness, and not the way?

Perhaps the waters of the Flood are *baptismal* waters, Wittgenstein says. Perhaps there are *joyful* names for the disaster …

We take our leave at his door.

How much time he has spent on his own!, Wittgenstein says.

No friends—not now, he's always said to himself. *Not until my work is done.*

But perhaps he has made friends, he says. Perhaps *we* are his friends.

Walking back to our rooms.

EDE: Did we save him, do you think? Have we done something good?

ME: I think we have. I think we did.

EDE: Why did we bother, I wonder?

ME: Because he was flagging. Because he needed us.

EDE: You're very tender, Peters. I hope you'll be around to save *me* when the time comes. (A pause.) My God, we've been sober for two whole days!

Ede's rooms. Titmuss arrives with a bottle of cognac; Doyle and Mulberry, with a bottle of absinthe.

Ede pours it all into a saucepan on the stove.

EDE: Gentlemen—did you know it's possible to *inhale* alcohol? It bypasses the stomach and goes straight to the lungs and brain. No need for the middleman. Digestion's strictly *old school*. You're supposed to use air pumps to vaporise it, and then pour it over dry ice. But I don't see why you can't just heat it and sniff.

We crowd round the saucepan, breathing deeply.

Delirium. Both Kirwins have passed out. Their hyper-fitness makes them vulnerable, we agree. A bit like Bruce Lee.

MULBERRY: The room's spinning.

DOYLE: My head's about to fall off.

MULBERRY: Ede, why are there two of you?

DOYLE (panicked): Help me! I think I'm going to die.

EDE: There's no way for the body to get rid of the alcohol. You can't vomit your way out of this one, Doyle. You'll just have to sit it out.

Titmuss launches into one of his India stories.

We lie, listening, in liquid-free drunkenness.

What a cliché Titmuss is!

Titmuss the India connoisseur. Titmuss moved by poverty

and staring peasants. Moved by being moved by poverty and staring peasants. Supposing himself to have learnt a *great Indian lesson*, and—worst of all!—supposing himself to have a great Indian lesson to teach!

Only three weeks in India, and a new Titmuss was born. A *heartfelt* Titmuss, unknown to friends and family. A *compassionate* Titmuss with tears of joy in his eyes, as happy as the saints of God ... A *great-souled* Titmuss, full of gap-year wisdom ... A *karmic* Titmuss, dreaming of the thousand incarnations of the Titmuss-soul before him—of Titmuss-slugs and Titmuss-bats and Titmuss-ground-sloths. An *eternal* Titmuss—born an amoeba, born an ant, working his way up to a pasty Cambridge student.

The next day. The Kirwins, running through the snow.

EDE: Do you think the Kirwins have ever known despair?

The Kirwins are too vigorous to have known despair, we agree. Unless they are vigorous *because* of their despair. Unless the Kirwins nurse some deeply buried *horror at life* from which they flee in triathlons and Ironman contests ...

The Kirwins' tragedy is that there's no war for them to die in, we agree. No chance of glory, no heroism. Ede imagines them charging some machine gun nest, without a thought for their safety. He sees Alexander Kirwin hurling back an enemy grenade, and Benedict Kirwin offering his body as a human shield to protect the soldiers behind him.

Of course, they could join up to fight in one of our stupid modern wars, Ede says. He imagines them blown up by roadside IEDs. But then, they'd learn to walk again on plastic legs, and salute visiting royalty with plastic arms, and enter the Paralympics, and head to the North Pole with Prince Harry. The Kirwins are irrepressible, Ede says.

The Kirwins will probably excel on the *corporate stage*, we agree. They'll work their way up to the boardroom. But they'll be haunted by a strange *emptiness*, we imagine—the same emptiness that makes them come to Wittgenstein's classes. And one will die in a supposed shooting accident (a gun pressed accidentally to his temple: how was *that* possible?). The other, shortly afterwards, will fly his light aircraft into an electricity pylon. They'll kill themselves without really knowing why ...

EDE: Have you seen their motivational phrases? (Reading

from the Kirwins' Facebook page:) *I can therefore I am. You are never too old to set another goal. If you can dream it, you can do it. By failing to prepare, you are preparing to fail. Either you run the day or the day runs you. Winners never quit and quitters never win. The harder the conflict, the more glorious the triumph. To begin, begin.*

Ede says we should post some de*motivational* phrases on our Facebook pages. *I can't therefore I am. To be is to be condemned. The universe is a mistake. Hope is a kind of delirium. We don't live even once. Dead days outnumber live ones. The use of philosophy is to sadden. Existence has never answered our questions. Death is the least of our problems.*

Wittgenstein's class. Thursday, three o'clock.

Silence. The hum of the computer. The cranking of an unbled radiator.

A poem on the board:

It is possible that to seem—is to be.
As the sun is something seeming and it is.
The sun is an example. What it seems
It is and in such seeming all things are.

There must be no more fundamental work in logic, Wittgenstein says. Logic must not be put on a proper footing. It is not a question of *helping logic to its feet*.

Logic must be *left to stumble*, he says.

Logic must suffer a *blow to the head*, he says. We must strike off the head of logic. No: we must strike off our *own* heads, if we are to do logic.

A form of life: that's what he's looking for, he says. A context in which his life would *make sense*.

Simply to stand with your feet upon the earth. Just to open your eyes. Just to be here—*here*. To be *of* God. *With* God. And no longer asking, *Why?*

A rose has no why. Ordinary life has no why. Isn't that what he's in search of: ordinary life, where the things themselves are right in front of us?

Our problem is that we want him to say something complicated, Wittgenstein says. But all he's concerned with is the obvious, the ordinary. All he's interested in is showing us what we already know.

DOYLE: But if we already know it, why is it so hard to understand?

WITTGENSTEIN: Because something stands between us and what we know. Because the obvious has become difficult to access. The obvious is not obvious *for us*, that's the trouble.

Friendly faces, Wittgenstein says, looking round the room at us. Faces to watch him as he tries to think. As he *fails* to think.

Once, love was the rule, and each one drew his neighbour upward, he quotes. Our faces, our very presence, draw him upward, he says. And perhaps, in his own way, he will draw *us* upward. Perhaps our presence will bring him the calm he needs, he says. Our presence, all of us around him, like a host of angels.

We are too *young* to hear him, he says. Too *innocent*. But he loves our youth, he says. He needs our innocence.

He must find *our* level, he says. He must put himself in *our* place, for his sake, if not for ours.

Pascal said that the true philosopher *makes light* of philosophy. He must try to learn from our lightness, Wittgenstein says. He must descend into our valleys.

Why is Chiron, the teacher of Achilles, presented as a centaur?, Wittgenstein asks—because the student must feel that the teacher is at a distance. A distance created by the presence of thought.

The teacher must be *higher* than the student, he says. A pause. No, that's not it. The teacher must bring the student into relationship with what is higher. Another pause. No, that is not it, either. And then: the teacher must suffer from his own lack of height, all the while consoling the student for *his* lack of height.

• • •

Socrates began thinking at whatever point his interlocutors were starting from. He accompanied them, travelled with them, until they came to their moment of crisis, when they were overwhelmed by discouragement and wanted to break off the discussion. And then—by what miracle?—Socrates would take his interlocutors' doubt and discouragement upon himself. And then—another miracle!—Socrates would *transfigure* this doubt, and *affirm* this confusion, until doubt and confusion became the *positive outcome* of philosophy.

Aporia, that's the word, Wittgenstein says, writing it on the blackboard. Literally—no passage, no way forward. *There exists a point of arrival, but no path*, he says, quoting. But perhaps there is no point of arrival, either.

A walk on the Backs.

We speak of the legendary *night-climbs* of Cambridge. Of St John's College Main Gate (easy—Doyle has climbed it on a drunken night out, he says). Of the Wren Library (very pretty, Alexander Kirwin says—he's climbed it twice). Of New Court Tower (he's stood on its peak before dawn, Benedict Kirwin says). And we speak of the famous Senate House leap, with its deadly plunge (Mulberry *wants* to plunge, he says).

Wittgenstein smiles. He likes listening to our nonsense, he says. He glories in our inanity! In the poverty of our prattle! It is like a balm to him. It is possible to *bathe* in nonsense, he says. To be *refreshed* by it.

We are his assistants, he says. His helpers. No, that's not it. For we do not really help him—we are more likely to get in his way. We are obstacles on his path. But we are *necessary* obstacles—obstacles placed there by God. Obstacles to remind him of lightness. Obstacles to show him that his way is too heavy—too arid, when it should be lightness itself; too dull, when it should flash and laugh and dazzle.

The path to thought lies also through laughter and forgetting: that is what we recall him to—that there must also be a *giddiness* of thought; that God Himself laughs; that God wants *us* to laugh ...

Christ's Pieces, after class. On the benches, Wittgenstein among us.

Guthrie performing Doyle's new show, based on the life of the *real* Wittgenstein.

Wittgenstein's visit to Bertrand Russell's Cambridge rooms (Guthrie expertly playing both men: Russell, languorous, relaxed, the English don, at ease in the world; Wittgenstein, frenetic, feverish, the Austrian intellectual, pacing the floor).

First song: 'Am I an Idiot, Or Just a Philosopher?' Sample lyric:

> *I knocked on Bertrand Russell's door*
> *Just before the First World War*
> *I said, Tell me, Sir, am I a real philosopher*
> *Or have you heard it all before?*

Wittgenstein's period as a soldier, hating his fellow soldiers, and possessed by the most terrible despairs (Guthrie's face an expressive miracle), but filled, too, with a new mysticism, a new religiosity (Guthrie's face luminous, God-touched) ...

Second song: 'Absolutely Safe.' Rousing chorus:

> *And when the enemy machine guns strafe*
> *God keeps me ... absolutely safe!*

Wittgenstein's break with philosophy—his period in the Austrian countryside, teaching peasant children, inspiring peasant children, but being over-severe with lazy peasant children. Wittgenstein, boxing their ears, spanking their backsides (Guthrie masterfully playing both Wittgenstein-the-teacher and the lazy pupils) ...

Third song: 'No One Understands Me.'

When I box the children's ears
It's just in order to still my fears
That they will grow up fearful slobs
And they will not believe in God ...

Wittgenstein's *architectural* period, designing and managing the building of a house for his sister. His extreme rigour, his eye for the smallest detail. And the uninhabitable home he constructed in the Bauhaus style, all severity, all sharp corners. (Guthrie's face an image of intensity, of focus, of exasperation ... Guthrie playing both Wittgenstein-the-architect, and his put-upon project manager, bursting into tears with stress ...)

Fourth song: 'Sharp Angles.'

Don't think I'm just acting
I'm not cruel, I'm just very exacting ...

Wittgenstein's return to Cambridge, not in triumph, but in humility. Philosophy, for him, now no longer a mapping of depth, but a topography of the surface (Guthrie, shoulders rounded, eyes to the floor).

Fifth song: 'Ordinary Life.'

I'm in love with ordinary life
I'll take the everyday as my wife

I prefer the chat of porter and bedmaker
To academic talk and the cocktail shaker ...

How Wittgenstein works! How he writes! (Guthrie miming the philosopher sitting at his desk, copying his remarks into an enormous ledger.) Wittgenstein, taking solitary Cambridge-hating walks (Guthrie, stomping, scowling). Wittgenstein, estranged from his colleagues (Guthrie, wagging his fingers, looking vexed). Wittgenstein, full of apocalyptic thoughts about the end of the world (Guthrie, hand to brow, shaking his head) ...

Wittgenstein, diagnosed with cancer. Wittgenstein, dying. Wittgenstein, speaking his last words (Guthrie, in swan-song brilliance).

Sixth song: 'A Wonderful Life.' As moving as Susan Boyle singing 'I Dreamed a Dream.' As Paul Potts doing 'Nessun Dorma.'

Tell them I had a wonderful life!
Tell them it was worth the strife!

Laughter, from Guthrie's fans. Even Wittgenstein smiles.

After philosophy, lightness will be the highest virtue, Wittgenstein says. Blitheness will be sought after above all things.

Divination: that's what he sees in our idiocy, he says. *Prophecy*. We are fragments of the future.

When the end of philosophy comes, we will weep, without knowing why we weep, he says. We will laugh, without knowing why we laugh. And as we weep, we will laugh. And as we laugh, we will weep ...

Mulberry and Doyle are modelling their relationship on George Michael and Kenny—free to fuck whoever they want; free to surf Grindr and cruise.

But Doyle's heart is not in it, he says—he just isn't promiscuous. Besides, he's too busy with the theatre. There are other things in life besides sex. But Mulberry ...

DOYLE (rolling his eyes): Well, you know what *he's* like.

Last night, Mulberry smoked crack on the roof of his house, Doyle says. Up on the roof, the ridge tiles between his thighs, laughing like a maniac, he declaimed a poem about a *coffin full of shit* ... Mulberry's obsessed with death, Doyle says. Even his laughter is tinged with death; even his laughing mouth is a pit of death ...

Nihilism: that's Mulberry's disease, Doyle says. A sense that nothing's really worth the candle. That the meaning of the world is vanishing. That all that is left are parodies of parodies of parodies. The blackest of black laughter. A laughter that laughs at itself, and laughs at itself laughing ... That all his laughter is laughter before a mirror ...

I've been possessed, Mulberry told Doyle last night. *I am legion. There's a horde of demons inside me, mocking me*, he said. *Laughing at me.*

Doyle reminded Mulberry of Wittgenstein's words. *We must not think about our thinking. We must not philosophise about philosophy. To know our dividedness, to state it, is to be divided yet further.* And when Mulberry climbed onto the roof, Doyle shouted up to him that we must not laugh at our laughter. But Mulberry was too high to hear.

E-mails from the Careers Service. Posters and flyers every-where, advertising the employers' fair. Recruitment agents, from the big City banks, from consultancies and law firms.

Brochures in our pigeonholes: *Your future starts now* (im-age: graduates throwing mortar boards in the air). *The career of your life starts here* (besuited trainees laughing with other trainees). *What if the next big thing is you?* (Godzilla-like grad-uate striding about). *Individuality rocks* (long-haired graduate playing a Flying V guitar). *Be more than just your job* (graduate sledding in the Arctic behind a team of huskies). *Grow further* (graduates in snorkels and flippers, exploring a coral reef). *Scale new heights* (free-climbing graduate, halfway up a cliff). *Apply if you want to go faster* (graduates on a down-plunging roller coaster). *Think big* (graduates in crampons crossing a ravine). *Are you extreme?* (parascending graduate, soaring into the sky). *We'll take you further than you imagine* (graduates slashing their way through the jungle).

We pass the time before class, translating the brochures. *Never manage to launch* (graduate back in childhood bedroom). *Earn nothing like the living wage* (graduate eating discount sandwich from *Boots*). *Never settle anywhere or at anything* (graduate with backpack, trudging city streets). *Join the intern nation* (graduate at the photocopier) …

The failure to launch. To leave your house. To leave your room. To leave your bed. To open your eyes in the morning. How easily it could happen! One mistimed bout of depression and that would be it—the rest of your life, in your parents' house, on soul-rotting medication.

We are nymphs, yet to shed our bodies. Yet to ascend fine-winged into life. But how easy it would be to slip and fall. How easy, to end up half-employed, underemployed, unemployed …

We feel as though the future were rummaging through us. Who knows what the future will find?

Wittgenstein, mystical today.

The *kairos* is coming, he says. The *end* is coming.

Time is gathered into itself like a wolf poised to leap upon its prey, he quotes.

He speaks of a new vocation of philosophy. A *revocation* of philosophy.

He speaks of philosophy practised *without* philosophy. Philosophy no longer subject to its own law.

He will have to *reawaken* philosophy, he says. He will have to conjure up *all* of its ghosts.

Philosophy must be reborn, he says. But *without itself*— without its substance.

He speaks of the time when we will have joyously forgotten philosophy. Forgotten what philosophy was *for*. A time when we will *play* with philosophy, like gods ...

We will not recognise him, after the end of philosophy, he says. We will not recognise each other!

Everything we have known, we will have forgotten. And when we remember it again, it will be in a new way.

You will leave Babylon with joy, he quotes. *You will be let out of the city in peace.*

After philosophy, no one will read, Wittgenstein says. And no one will stop reading. It will be impossible to distinguish reading from looking, from glancing, from letting your eyes rest on one sight or another.

After philosophy, no one will write, he says. And no one will stop writing. The merest gesture will be a kind of writing. A cough. A hairstyle. The flight of birds: all writing.

And *after philosophy*, there will be no more teaching, only learning, he says. No more studying, only encountering. No more classrooms, only walks along the Backs ...

Walking home. Okulu ahead of us on the path, massive head-phones over his ears. Faint strains of Mozart. A one-man protest against *Cambridge superficiality*.

We *disappoint* Okulu, we know that. He wants something from us. *Seriousness. Depth.* He wants to discuss ideas. But we let him down.

Okulu is like a *reverse missionary*, we agree. Like one of those Anglican priests, come from former colonies to re-evangelise us. Only it's not religion Okulu brings, but *culture*—old culture, high culture. Okulu is a high priest of old culture ...

Okulu is a man of taste. Of cultivation. And Okulu *knows* things—about current affairs, about the latest philosophical and scientific theories. But about the *past*, too. He's been seen in the library, with piles of old hardbacks ...

But who needs libraries? Who needs books? We have them on our e-readers. Or rather, we *could have* them. We *could have* anything at all. Everything from the past can be called up in the present. Everything can be here—everything that was ever thought, or written, or composed, or painted. We *can* commune with all the ghosts. We *can* wake up the dead. But who wants to wake up the dead?

Library hardbacks *should* stay closed, their secrets hidden. Their spines should stay turned to us on their shelves. Keep them asleep. We won't disturb them. They're not for us, after all. They were not written *with us in mind*.

And they reek of the past. Their pages have the musty smell

of the past. The smell of old forgotten things. Of things that should be forgotten. Sun-browned pages. Date-stamps from decades ago. Annotations in a tiny hand. Underlinings. Whole passages marked in yellow highlighter. Tan-brown stains from coffee and tea. Evidence of squashed insects. Dried-up tear splashes. Curly strands of pubic hair. Traces of wiped blood. Mementos: an old train ticket, a cinema ticket ... Old things! Old things!

The old world is passing. Worlds and worlds are vanishing. A whole civilisation—that was once *our* civilisation—sinks into the greeny-black depths of forgetting ...

Poor, mournful Okulu of the library stacks ... Poor deep-diving Okulu. He, like us, is seeking a past that grows ever more remote. He, like us, is a creature of the upper waters—of the sun-suffused shallows. But he, unlike us, hasn't forgotten the depths ...

Next year, a new crop of students will appear to replace us. Next year, our tutors will already have begun to forget us. Our essays and exam scripts will be shredded and recycled. Our photos will disappear from internal websites. Our academic referees will no longer be sure who we were. We'll be confused with this person, with that one. And in the end, we'll be lost in the anonymous crowd of all the students who were ever taught here.

We each bear a trace of every student who ever studied at Cambridge. We are each a ghost of all the other students— students who have been here, and students who have yet to be here. Our lecturers, who will have seen us already, will see us again. We will have been here before, for our lecturers. We will be here again. There is neither end nor beginning.

But with Wittgenstein it is different. We are not nobodies. We are not insignificant. We are at Cambridge for a reason: that's what his presence helps us to believe. We are here *for him*, just as he is here *for us*. And we are here, Wittgenstein and his men, for the sake of *thought*.

Something is happening. Something is going on that *will not be repeated.*

The *convolutions* of his lectures. How complex his enemy is!, he says. How complex, then, his classes must be!

Is it necessary, in some way, to recapitulate the entire history of philosophy in his lectures?, he wonders. The entire history of philosophical *mistakes*?

Is it necessary to lead his class to the origins of philosophy? Is it necessary to lead us to an *originary philosophical bafflement*?

Katargesis: written on his blackboard in capital letters. And in small letters, below: *The fulfilment of the Law. Fulfilment* underlined. Then, in still smaller letters: *The fulfilment of philosophy??* Two question marks. *The end of philosophy???* Three question marks.

What will he say when the last words of philosophy are spoken?, Wittgenstein wonders. What will he say, when the spell of philosophy has been broken?

He'll say nothing, he says. He'll open his eyes. He'll look up at the sky. He'll laugh.

After philosophy, thoughts will be common, Wittgenstein says. Thought will belong to all, like the sunlight, like the rain.

After philosophy, there will be nothing important at all, he says—*everything* will be important. *Everything* will take on significance. The light on a particular afternoon will be as rich as the collected works of Kant.

·   ·   ·

To come across philosophy rusting in a field, like an old piece of farm machinery. To chance upon philosophy as one might the fossilised carcass of some great prehistoric beast. That's what he wants, he says. To *decommission* philosophy. To place it *out of use*, as former terrorists do their weapons ...

For two and a half thousand years, philosophy has been turning like a cat, wanting to lie down. Two and a half thousand years of thought seeking rest, seeking sleep, seeking death ...

But soon thought will lie down, he says. Soon, philosophy will lie down.

Only at its end will we know what philosophy was, he says. Only at the brink of its cessation will philosophy reveal itself.

On the last day, philosophy will stand silhouetted against non-philosophy. Against the *storms* of non-philosophy.

On the last day, thought will lie down with the opposite of thought. On the last day, thought and the world will be as one.

On the last day, *there will be nothing left to think*. On the last day, thought itself will become redundant.

At the end, after the end, we will use the *Critique of Pure Reason* as a kilo-weight, the *Tractatus* as scrap paper. Our children will doodle on the works of Plato, and make paper boats from the pages of Spinoza. They will fold the *Monadology* into a paper hat ...

The end of logic. The end of philosophy.

His head will empty, when it comes, he says. His head will be empty, as our heads are *already* empty.

And philosophy will be revealed as what it is, and what it always was—*nothing*. And logic will have at last *come into its own*—as *nothing*.

The end will see the hollowing-out of philosophy, he says. The *voiding* of logic. Until it becomes the empty shell through which nothingness roars like a distant sea.

Three AM. The hard white light of Accident and Emergency. Guthrie, propped between Ede and I, apparently concussed. Staging the death of Empedocles was bound to have its risks.

An indignant rah, demanding to be attended to *straight away*. A suicidal Sloane, wheeled straight into resus. A Varsity face, moaning loudly, a patch over his right eye. Some rugby beefcake bluelighted in after a drinking game—*it's not a good night unless you end up in A&E*, he bellows.

EDE (pissed off): I wish he'd fucking shut up—fucking caveman.

Cries as minor fractures are set. As local anaesthetic is injected. Groaning. Wailing. The malty smell of urine.

The doctor shines a light in Guthrie's eye, and disappears again.

EDE (more pissed off): Fuck this.

We stare at the *no-win, no-fee* solicitors' notices. At the in-house hospital magazine. At the *ward philosophy* poster—*striving for your health in a holistic way ... encompassing your disabilities ... understanding your cultural sensitivities ...*

EDE (completely pissed off): Let's just leave him here, for fuck's sake. He won't know the difference.

GUTHRIE/EMPEDOCLES: *Can't you see where you are looking? You see the earth, a pit, and you see only these miserable laws, which are laws of the dead. Don't you look to the laws of the gods?*

We prop Guthrie against the wall. Snatches of Empedocles follow us to the door.

· · ·

Out—into the night. The sense of having made the greatest of escapes.

Our friendships are not deep, we agree. We hardly know what friendship means. We happen to come together, that's all. We coincided, that's all. We were going in the same direction for a while, and we made the best of it.

Cambridge is only an interlude, we agree. Cambridge is a corridor, a passageway. And we've milled about together, waiting for life to begin.

After Cambridge, we'll fall out of contact. After Cambridge, we'll unfriend each other on Facebook. After Cambridge, we'll forget each other's names. Each other's voices. After Cambridge, we'll begin to confuse each other with someone else.

We fell into step with one another for a while, that is all. *We passed the time . . .*

The Snowball.

Ede and I, in our dress suits, knocking on Wittgenstein's door.

He looks tall when he answers. Neat. No jacket. White shirt. Pleated trousers, worn high on the waist.

How fresh his room seems! His floor—how it shines! I picture myself walking across it in bare feet.

WITTGENSTEIN (smiling): Your ties are all wrong.

He reaches out just as Ede lifts his chin, adjusting the angle of Ede's bow tie.

How intense he is! As though bow ties were a problem in logic!

WITTGENSTEIN (smiling again): There!

My turn. I look upwards, at the panelling on the ceiling.

WITTGENSTEIN: That's better. Now, off you go and lose your souls.

Bubble machine and bouncy castle …

Girls in ball gowns, leaping in their tights. Rahs in dinner jackets, jumping in their socks.

And whooping. Everybody whooping. It's quite the new thing, whooping.

This would be the right moment for a *campus massacre*, we agree.

· · ·

Cocaine. Tequila. More cocaine. More tequila. Our noses tingle. Our throats are hoarse from shouting. Our heads are dizzy ...

The entertainment arrives: children's TV presenters, reality TV stars. *Are we all having a good time tonight? Have we all been good boys and girls? Have we written our lists for Santa? Have we gobbled up all the chocolates in our advent calendars?*

More cocaine and tequila, to numb the pain. Have we all taken quite enough drugs and alcohol?

Doyle's come as Bad Santa, and Mulberry, as his demonic elf, with a sack full of laughing gas balloons. We whoop ourselves crazy ...

The park, 3.00 AM. Titmuss, lying in the flowers, chanting quietly. Guthrie, in Doyle's Santa hat, kebab grease around his mouth. Ede and I on the bench, sharing a bottle of vodka.

EDE: He likes you.

ME: Who?

EDE: Wittgenstein. Wittgenstein likes you.

ME: What do you mean, *likes me?*

EDE: I mean *likes* you, you idiot. It's obvious.

ME: Fuck off. No way.

EDE: It's your boyish charm. Your innocence. You really are an innocent, Peters.

ME: There's no way he likes me.

EDE (sagely, draining the last of the vodka): That's why he likes you, Peters: because you say things like that.

In my dream, snow falls on Wittgenstein's sleeping body. Snow covers him, like a crisp white bedroom sheet. But it covers his shoulders and his arms and his head, too.

In my dream, he is stirring, his eyes are opening. His head falls to one side. He's facing—*me*.

In my dream, his eyes plead. His mouth moves, but I cannot hear what he says.

In my dream, I wipe the snow from his brow. I wipe it from his body.

In my dream, I kneel at his side, like a supplicant.

King Street, then Park Street. Ede and I, a bottle of gin in each pocket.

We've outgrown this place, we agree. We're sick of it. We've explored the lanes, we've walked the courtyards. We've seen behind the high walls and the iron doors.

How many times have we drunk ourselves silly in the *Maypole*? How many times have we scavenged for alcohol after closing time? How many times have we raided the communal kitchens last thing at night? How many times have we pissed in our sinks? How many times have we stepped over vomit? How many times have we done an all-night essay blitz, high on energy drinks and Pro Plus tablets?

We're bored. Bored of study. Bored of preparing for life. Bored of waiting for life to begin.

ME: There's one thing for sure—I'm not taking a fucking gap year!

EDE: Fuck gap years! Reality! That's what we need! We need to know what we're up against!

The high street. Office workers out for their Christmas parties. Women in round-toed high heels and maxi dresses and ankle bracelets. Men in Fred Perry shirts ...

EDE: That's you next year, Peters—Fred Perry shirt, and a look of damnation ...

We imagine my office-job future. Office rivalries. Office flirtations. Conversations about cars. And football. And last night's TV. Watching the clock. Wandering the corridors. Cold-calling clients on a Saturday morning. Telemarketing on a Sunday night. Pulling all-nighters to impress the boss. Out on the town with people I can't stand. Saving up for a starter house in an exurb. Hanging myself in the company toilets.

EDE: Not to worry, Peters. It won't be much better for me ...

He's going to be one of the *bad* Edes, Ede says. These are probably his last weeks of lucidity. He's going to go the way of Guthrie. The way of Scroggins. Drunk every night by cocktail hour. Then rehab. Then interventions. Then *360s*. Then suicide attempts. Then electroshock treatment. Then, finally, a shotgun to the head.

EDE (at the top of his voice): Fuck this!

ME (louder): FUCK THIS!

Only one more term to go. Only one more. The world is rushing to meet us. The world is crowding our vision. The world is flaming towards us, like a comet. When will it strike? When will it burst across our skies?

Terrible, decisive things are about to happen. Knives are glittering in the darkness. *Teeth* are glittering in the darkness. The night, the whole night, is opening wide.

We're so vulnerable! So exposed! We're drowning in possibility. In potential.

We're lost in time. Lost *to* time. We're abandoned to the wilds of time. Wandering in time's night ...

Last class before the Christmas break. Wittgenstein brings us Lebkuchen and wine.

He talks softly, as he always does. His intent, after all, is so utterly at odds with loudness. But today, his voice drops almost to a whisper.

An old Jewish legend tells that there are nine righteous people alive in the world at any moment, Wittgenstein says— but he likes to imagine there are *nine righteous thinkers*— thinkers who will know what it means for philosophy to have ended.

Nine righteous thinkers, who will know the burden that has been lifted … Nine last seers, who will feel the *relief* of the end, who will know themselves to have been unburdened from thinking and from the task of thinking …

Nine last logicians, who will be free to walk out beneath the summer sun … Nine last visionaries, who will emerge, blinking, from their thinking-shacks and thought-burrows … Nine righteous ones, who will open their eyes at last, who will breathe the air to the bottom of their lungs …

Nine righteous philosophers, who will *laugh* at last—who will really laugh, like children … Nine righteous thinkers, who only now will step into life, into the fullness of life.

A last walk on the Backs. Wittgenstein ahead, in deep discussion with Okulu.

Ede and I, light-headed from the wine …

We imagine the *righteous Inuit*, a virtuoso of despair, thinking about thinking as she crosses the dark ice on her snowmobile. Soon, the sun will rise for the first time in six months. Soon, the *post-philosophical* sun will rise. Soon, there will come the post-philosophical *dawn* ...

We imagine the *righteous Siberian*, eyes bloodshot, ruined by alcohol. Ruined by *philosophy*. Downing a quart of vodka every morning before breakfast, to be done with his thoughts. Soon, the bottle will fall from his hands. Soon, he will reach a new kind of drunkenness, a new kind of *sobriety* ...

We imagine the *righteous sannyasin*, a profound cousin of Chakrabarti, having died to the world, having condemned himself to wander until the end of philosophy. Soon, he will arrive at his destination. Soon, he will realise that he has already arrived; that the world, his place of exile, is everywhere his *home* ...

We imagine the *righteous mental patient*, zoned out on meds. Half awake for years, blurry-headed for years, but knowing that soon, it will be time to throw away her tranquilisers— that soon, it will be time to exit the asylum, and be welcomed in the world as the prodigal sister, the measure of sanity ...

We imagine the *righteous pair of philosopher-saints*, living at the edges of the Egyptian desert. Philosopher-lovers, completing each other's thoughts, each other's sentences. Soon, they'll kiss away philosophy. Soon, very soon, they'll weep away philosophy ...

We imagine the *righteous AI*, blinking into consciousness, thinking electronic thoughts in Bell Laboratories. And, in a nanosecond, exhausting every philosophical move. Every *existential* move ... Soon, it will sink back into blissful nonconsciousness. Soon, it will rejoin the inanimate world ...

We imagine the *righteous philosopher-dolphin*, diving

through the waves—wanting only to love diving through the waves, wanting only to love the sun on its back ... Soon, it will be reunited with the elements. Soon, it will be no more than a part of the sea, diving through the sea ...

We imagine *God Himself*, Wittgenstein's God, born of torment as the opposite of torment, born of pain as the opposite of pain, knowing that the time has come to vacate His throne. Soon, divinity will be reborn on earth. Soon, the godhead will show itself in the sky ...

Grantchester meadows.

Ede proposes we create a *living orrery*.

Chakrabarti is the earth. Okulu, the moon, begins an orbit around him. Then Chakrabarti and Okulu begin to orbit Guthrie, the sun.

Doyle/Mercury runs rapidly round Guthrie, and Ede/Venus does the same a little farther out, but both inside Chakrabarti/Earth's trajectory. I am Mars, running in a wider circle, and Mulberry is the asteroid belt. Alexander Kirwin is Deimos, and Benedict Kirwin, Phobos: Mars's moons, orbiting me tightly. Titmuss, zigzagging through the grass, stands in for all the outer planets.

A laughing solar system, with laughing planets and laughing moons, and Guthrie in the middle, the great laughing sun. And even Wittgenstein laughs—even his wintry face breaks into laughter.

After philosophy, we will be as children at play, he says. Any seriousness will be *put-on* seriousness. Any solemnity will be *playful* solemnity.

. . .

We walk back along the river. Mulberry, stripped to his *MES-SIAH* T-shirt, carrying Doyle on his shoulders. Guthrie, flush-faced, walking on his hands. The Kirwins, all muscle, in matching rowing vests, shouting and laughing. Chakrabarti, in deep conversation with Ede. Titmuss, flowers in his dreads, chanting *om*. And Wittgenstein at our head, beaming.

Cambridge opens to us as to Christ and his disciples.

After philosophy, the *fact* of Cambridge will overwhelm us, Wittgenstein says. The *fact* that it is, that it even exists.

After philosophy, we will lose our way in Cambridge, he says. The most familiar streets will become unknown.

After philosophy, Cambridge will *hatch*. The walls of the colleges will crack like eggshells ...

After philosophy, the suburbs and exurbs will crumble, and the new developments will return to grass. *After philosophy*, the hideous buildings will fall down one by one ...

4

Saturday. End of term. Parents come to collect their offspring. The open boots of cars packed with things—with Anglepoise lamps, with bicycles, with rolled-up posters, with pots of cacti … Boarding school all over again.

A last walk with Ede.

EDE: So you're really staying on?

ME: I'm staying on.

EDE: Do you really expect to be able to help him?

ME: I want to be here when he calls.

EDE: Peters! Help me *mit mein lederhosen!*

Farewells on the steps. Hugs. See-you-laters. Saying goodbye like World War II fighter pilots. *Well, this is it, old man. Cheerio, old chap. Take care now. Goodbye, old sock. Toodle-oo, old thing. Chocks away, groover. Chin-chin, old pal!* Goodbye for six weeks, until the new term in January. Goodbye, until the new calendar year.

TITMUSS (pressing his palms together in a Hindu gesture): *Namaste.*

I embrace Chakrabarti in a rush of spurious emotion. Safe journey home, old chap. And goodbye to Guthrie. Goodbye to the Kirwins! To Okulu! Goodbye, goodbye, goodbye.

The campus, deserted.

The colleges, hired out for conferences, on every topic under the sun. Dental Hygiene. Phospholipids. Phage Display. Entrepreneurial Innovation. Angel Investors. Process Design. Tapeworm Infrastructure ...

A handful of tourists, dressed up against the cold. A few dedicated postgraduates, in Moon Boots and puffa jackets ...

Snow, in drifts. A frozen River Cam. The sky, blue and cold and far. Cambridge, as Scandinavia. Cambridge, at the North Pole.

Monday comes. Then Tuesday. Then Wednesday.

A text from Wittgenstein. *Please come. Am unwell.*

I buy a bag of scones from the patisserie, and clotted cream and jam from *Sainsbury's*.

He looks ill, in his armchair, with his flannel pyjamas and his dressing gown, and his hair in disarray.

I make tea in his kitchen. A metal teapot. A tin for loose leaves. An enamel tray.

He's had fever for a week, he says.

On his desk, tiny slivers of paper. Trimmings from a photograph, of a young woman at a piano with her eyes closed. His mother, he says.

Picture-taking is a sacred thing, he says. It should be like *learning to see*. It should take a great mental *effort*. That's why he's trimming his photo, he says—he's trying to learn how to see.

For the Kabbalists, beauty was once a golden whole, which then shattered, he says. But it isn't so. Beauty is real. Beauty is here. It is *we* who have shattered.

Next day. Another text. *Do come again.*

Up the staircase, with another bag of scones. He wears a chunky sweater, like a '60s folk singer.

He serves tea.

His hands are refined. Not delicate, exactly. *Wise.* A *philosopher's* hands.

To be touched by those hands ... To be held by those hands ...

He's been reading Augustine's *Confessions*, he says—the most serious book ever written.

It's not as if Augustine has anything *dreadful* to confess, Wittgenstein says. It's not as if Augustine was a murderer. He is really only *typically* sinful.

Augustine's distinction lies in his *awareness* of his sin, Wittgenstein says. He is aware of it as others are not. He has the *capacity* for awareness, as others do not. This is what makes him more sinful—*extra* sinful.

His voice drops to a whisper. *He* dreams of confession, he says. Of simply *showing* his sins. Even the sin of *self-consciousness*, he says—barely audible.

After philosophy, everything will be shown, he says. There will be no shadows. *After philosophy*, there will be a name for everything, and not just for every *kind* of thing.

After philosophy, we will have learnt the art of reading faces, he says. There will be no secrets. Our inner lives will be open to all, like glassfish.

After philosophy, the dark side of the moon will turn to face us.

He texts after lunch. Need to wash off brain. A film? Something trashy?

Pretty Woman, showing at the *Kino*. He sits up close to the screen, wholly absorbed. He laughs and claps his hands at the final scene. The snow-white limo, necktie tied to the aerial like a knight's colours. *La Bohème* blaring. Richard Gere standing through the sunroof, a bunch of roses in his hand, waving. Julia Roberts on the fire escape, letting down her hair. Richard Gere clambering up, sweeping her into his arms, kissing her ...

RICHARD GERE: What did the princess do when her knight came to rescue her?

JULIA ROBERTS: She rescued him right back.

We walk back through the snow in silence, following the great walls of the colleges.

Do I know what he said to himself when he came here?, Wittgenstein asks.

I will do such things—

What they are, yet I know not, but they shall be the terrors of the earth.

And what *did* he do? He smiles. The walls did not come tumbling down. Everything remains exactly the same. Cambridge is Cambridge is Cambridge ...

He speaks of the Cambridgean *void*. Of the Cambridgean

nothingness. He speaks of the Cambridgean *emptying-out.* Of the Cambridgean *hollowing.*

He speaks of *eroded hours* and *emptied-out days.* He speaks of *time void of time*—of minutes, of seconds. Nothing is happening, not in Cambridge, he says. Nothing is happening—rubble is piling upon rubble, and that is all.

Cambridge is a *shore*, he says. A shore, waiting for a sea. When will the sea crash in and reclaim the Fens? When will the flood come that will drown Cambridge?

8th December

Carollers in the courtyard. The vast Christmas tree—a present from Norwegian alumni.

The Hasidim say that everything in the world to come will be almost as it is in this world, Wittgenstein says. Just as the Christmas tree is now, so will it be then. Where the carollers sing now, so they will sing then. The gloves and hat we wear in this world, those we will wear then. Everything will be as it is now, only a little different ...

A package for him at the porters' lodge. He picks up a package. It's from his aunt, he says.

Stollen and sparkling wine in his rooms.

Wittgenstein, in buoyant mood. He speaks of his childhood. Of his parents. His brother. He speaks of the mountains. Of long horseback rides through the valleys.

He lost his faith early on, he says—or what is usually called faith. He remembers a school trip, when he was still very young. It was dark, and they were walking back home through a forest. Some of the other children were frightened, and began to cry. *You must think about God very hard*, the teacher said.

A few years later, he remembers wanting to fall on his knees, Wittgenstein says. There was a tiny church halfway up a mountain. Very simple, very beautiful. He wanted to pray, but he couldn't pray. He wanted to weep, but he couldn't do that, either. If he'd started to weep, he'd never have stopped, he says. He has the same feeling today.

There was a fairy story his mother used to tell them, he says. A wicked witch placed a splinter of ice in the heart of a boy. The boy forgot his parents and his name. He forgot the land of his birth. The witch carried him to her ice palace in the far north, and gave him a puzzle of ice shards to play with.

But the boy had a brother, who had not forgotten him. The brother found the ice palace, and the blue-lipped boy, lost in his puzzle. The brother embraced the boy, and the boy wept, without knowing why. And that is when the splinter of ice in his heart melted. That's when he remembered who he was. That's when he remembered his brother and his parents and the land of his birth ...

God is a name for tears—fresh *tears*, Wittgenstein says. God is a name for the act of weeping ...

Is it only by weeping, *really* weeping, that he will drive the splinter of philosophy from his heart?, he wonders.

9th December

We walk through the snow, to the American cemetery.

Be ye also ready, on one headstone. *Seek me and ye shall live*, on another. *Bound together by His love*, on a third.

Some cemeteries have no headstones, he says. Only a single churchyard cross, to mark the resting places of the dead. He finds that moving, he says—relinquishing your worldly name as monks do when they take the names of their saintly forebears.

He and his brother used to pass St Mary's monastery, near their home. They used to watch the monks working together— digging in the garden and pruning fruit trees. Once, they saw them singing vespers in the fields. How he envied them!

Spiritual poverty!, he says. To renounce possession of your own soul, your own will. To be poor, but to have God as your fortune ...

Perhaps the secret of life is not hidden, he says. Perhaps the secret of life is to work with others. *Alongside* others. To work in the fields, in the open air. The simple round of prayer and labour and reading ... Day after day ... Like a waterwheel in the river of eternity.

He attended services a few times, he says. So early, the stone vaulting was lost in shadows. Monks were scarcely visible in the gloom. And then dawn came, he says ... the first rays shining into the apse. Hope! Living hope! Prefiguring the return of Christ.

He dreams of building his life again from rituals, he says. Of remaking his life, action by action. Of beginning again, simply. Of concentrating on small things. On ordinary things.

10th December

He texts me: *come.—Coming.*

His door is slightly ajar.

He sits on his chair, head back, eyes half closed. Is he working on something? A philosophical problem? A *moral* problem? Has he fallen asleep?

WITTGENSTEIN (imperatively, his eyes still closed): Peters—take dictation. (Without pausing:) The rule must be a thread in the weave of life. The rule must become the exception, and the exception, the rule. (A pause.) Are you getting all this?

He speaks, I write. He doesn't open his eyes until lunchtime.

Afternoon. He serves coffee and cream, with biscuits. He's in a good mood after the day's work.

WITTGENSTEIN: You mustn't think I'm taking you for granted, Peters. (A pause.) I may be a wicked person (ME: You're not!), but I have always been a collector of good people.

ME: I've always thought you'd find me stupid.

WITTGENSTEIN: You, Peters, are anything but stupid.

How tired he is of Cambridge cleverness!, he says. He would prefer an honest stupidity—a *bright* stupidity, on which light shines from above.

• • •

The *Maypole*, almost empty.

A student at the next table tries to engage us in conversation. Something about Library Whispers. About the May Ball. At last, he leaves.

WITTGENSTEIN: Why did you talk to that fellow, Peters? He was a fool. (A pause.) You should tender yourself more dearly.

An influx of thesps, after some event at the ADC. Foppish cherubs with classical curls; shabby-posh Withnails in worn-shiny velvet; would-be Footlighters in comedy onesies.

Wittgenstein blanches. There is something despicable about theatre, he says.

Still more students. Comprehensive-school types, visibly unhealthy. Indie kids, with pipe-cleaner legs. Empiricist boys, with ruler-straight fringes. Big brainy girls, with glasses and headbands.

WITTGENSTEIN: Socrates's greatness was that he could talk with ordinary people, and consider such talk worthwhile. *My* greatness should be that I can spend an evening in the *Maypole* and find that evening worthwhile.

He stands. Puts on his coat.

WITTGENSTEIN: I am not great, Peters.

11th December

Busy, he texts.

12th December

Towards the Backs.

Frozen grass. An ice-covered slide. The words *fuck* and *piss*, written into the snow.

He went to the college Christmas party last night, he says. It was worse than he feared.

The head of the college, circulating. Her husband, circulating. Their grown-up children, circulating. Guests, circulating, circulating, circulating.

It used to be all *Cambridge stuffiness*, he says. All *Cambridge snobbery*. But it's all *friendliness* now, he says. All *openness* and *affability*. All *first names*. As though everyone were *mates*.

The buildings of Cambridge Riverside. A clutter of balconies. High, blank windows.

He wants an enemy, he says. A betrayer. One to bring the wrath of the university upon him. A Judas, to bring the anger of the *dons* upon his head.

He wants a *reckoning*, he says. Him versus Cambridge. He wants to *draw Cambridge out*. To be seen to sin against Cambridge. To have transgressed Cambridge. He wants a sense that there are limits. That there are things which are intolerable.

He wants to be handed over to the authorities. He wants to be *a case to be dealt with*.

The river.

Once, there were *disputes* at Cambridge, he says. Once, there were enmities between dons. This one wouldn't speak to that one; this one would leave the room when that one entered; this one would denounce the theories of that one in his lectures, and have his theories denounced in his turn.

Once, there were schools of thought in continual dispute. Once, there were debates about methodology. About legitimacy. About the very notion of philosophy. Once, there were old rivalries between Cambridge colleges, and between Cambridge and Oxford, and between Cambridge and Oxford and the rest of the world.

But it's all smiles now, he says.

They think they are kind. But they are not kind. They think they are right. But they are not right. They think that theirs is the only world. But theirs is not the only world. They think their world is the best of all possible worlds. But theirs is not the best of all possible worlds ...

The enemy does not understand that it is the enemy, that is the problem, he says. The enemy does not understand that it could be the enemy. The enemy does not grasp its own invidiousness. Its own *horror*. It is the good conscience of the enemy that makes it the enemy, he says. Its smugness. Its *Who me?* innocence.

Riverside Place. Overblown, glitzy.

He has the sense that he's on trial, he says. That he's waiting for a sentence to be handed down. For a judgement. For things to be decided. Only nothing is decided. And no judgement is handed down. That is his punishment.

His torture is the very *absence* of torture, he says. His punishment, the very *absence* of punishment. Which means that no one recognises his pain. That no one can understand his pain.

They would not even call his pain *pain*, he says. They would not allow his suffering to be *suffering*. The *pain* of pain; the *suffering* of suffering: he is denied even them.

In Cambridge, his path would be the right path *even if it were the wrong path*, he says. He would be in the right *even if he were wrong*, and perhaps *especially* if he were wrong.

St Bartholomew's Court. Toytown.

How he would have loved to have made a speech!, he says. A Christmas party lecture. A yuletide monologue.

We must revive the notion of *sin*, he would have said. Of *shame*. Of *guilt*. We must revive the need for *humiliation* and *mortification*.

We must *declare war on ourselves*, he would have said. We must be *fanatics*. *Fundamentalists*.

Ruthlessness, that is what is demanded of us, he would have said. *Cruelty*. And we must be cruel to ourselves first of all. We must be ruthless with ourselves.

It is too late to temper our views, he would have said. Too late to compromise.

They are *thought-investors*, he would have told them. *Thought-speculators. Hedge-fund-thinkers.*

They *belong* to Cambridge, he would have told them. They *deserve* Cambridge.

They are *bollards—human bollards*, he would have told them. The intellectual equivalents of suburban cul-de-sacs and out-of-town retail parks.

But he knows they would only have smiled, he says. He knows they would only have applauded.

A bench, sheltered from the snow. He slumps down, like a wounded man.

Cambridge is throttling him, he says. Cambridge is murdering him.

I put my hand on his back, and then my arm round his shoulders. He leans into me.

13th December

His rooms.

Snow turns to rain outside.

His work is not going well, he says.

He used to have nightmares of waking up in a coffin, he says. Of being buried alive in a coffin, and futilely scratching at the roof of his coffin.

He has woken up in the coffin of philosophy. His thought—his entire philosophical life—has been a futile scratching at the roof of his coffin.

Philosophy is a deluge, he says. Philosophy is rain, constantly falling.

Philosophy, always more philosophy, pouring over the ground already waterlogged with philosophy.

To come *after* something, and *before* nothing: that's our condition, he says. To have come *too late*, and not really to know it. Not really to understand *what it is that we are too late for.*

Silence.

WITTGENSTEIN: How can my company be interesting for you?

I laugh.

WITTGENSTEIN: Am I not a kind of *monster?*

I laugh again.

WITTGENSTEIN: We are like beauty and the beast. (Silence.) I am more corrupt than anyone I know.

ME: Why are you always so serious!?

WITTGENSTEIN: Life is serious.

A long pause.

WITTGENSTEIN (looking at me): Help me, Peters.

I tell him I don't know how to help him.

He speaks of his loneliness. Of his isolation. He speaks of his *animal desire for warmth*. Of his human desire for a *friendly face*.

Once, he believed a bell would sound through his loneliness, he says. That the pitch of his loneliness would reach a kind of *purity* ...

But that was when he believed in his work. In his *Logik*. That was when he thought he was on the brink of the great Solution. It's when he dreamt of a *sanctified* logic. Of a *logic of the temple*. It's when he dreamt that philosophy itself was calling out for help from him. And now ... He shakes his head.

The meaning of life consists in living that life, he says. But how is that possible: to *live life*? How would it be possible *for him*?

Silence. He stares at me for a full minute.

Madness is coming, he says. *His* madness is coming.

Madness will stroke his hair, and whisper in his ear.

Madness will say, *Do not be afraid.*

But he is afraid, he says.

Silence.

WITTGENSTEIN: You are my friend, aren't you?

ME: I am your friend.

WITTGENSTEIN: Help me, Peters.

14th December

We walk through the streets. I am to talk, he says. He is sick of the sound of his own voice.

I chatter about Ede drinking his way through his father's wine cellar. About Scroggins, on the waiting list for the world's first artificial bladder. I tell him of the Kirwins, who are on safari (Ede hopes they'll get eaten, I say—Wittgenstein smiles). I tell him about boarding school. About my poetry. I tell him about lambing. About buzzards. About boxing hares. I tell him about not knowing what to do with my life.

King's College Chapel.

The sound of choristers practising for a Christmas concert. He stands, rapt, no longer attending to my prattle. It's unbelievable, he says. Such beauty!

He speaks of the *daimonia* in music. Of music's eternal strangeness. He speaks of the melting of language into song. Of pure music, foreign to truth, to morality, to reason . . .

Plato feared music—the *power* of music, Wittgenstein says. And Plato was right. Music is foreign to us. Music is greater than we are. More *innocent.*

There is such a thing as a *roaring* innocence, Wittgenstein says. Such a thing as a *terrible* innocence.

He's afraid of music, he says. And for the same reason, he's afraid of *me.*

I don't understand. What does he mean?

. . .

The Backs, Wittgenstein's arm in mine.

He speaks of the *Confessions*.

Augustine writes as a sinner, he says. His story is not one of triumph. His story is of weakness and uncertainty.

Shadows press upon Augustine, he says. Chaos invades Augustine's heart …

He too fears chaos, Wittgenstein says. *He too* fears the *wilderness of the soul*.

But perhaps the miracle of repentance is close, he says. Perhaps there really can be such a thing as a *change of heart*.

Later, at his door. A kiss goodbye. And another. And another.

The echo of his footsteps, going upward.

15th December

Wittgenstein's rooms.

Dictation. At least ten pages. I don't understand a word.

He seems aggressive in his thought. Almost violent. He speaks in lunges. In stabs. But he is quickly exhausted.

Long silences, with occasional remarks about sin. About illness. About philosophy.

Behind the mystique of philosophy: nothing, I write. *Behind the mystique of the philosopher: likewise, nothing. In the end, we can say no more than that which everyone knows*, I write.

WITTGENSTEIN: You must go away from me. Or I must go away from you.

ME: No. Why?

WITTGENSTEIN: I am changing you. Corrupting you.

ME: You're *helping* me!

WITTGENSTEIN: It only seems like that. (A pause.) What will you become, if you stay with me?

Silence. Snow falling in large flakes.

I place my hand on his. I stroke his hand with mine.

He will have to transform himself, if he is to be worthy of me, he says. God will have to change him.

But he fears he cannot transform himself. And he fears he cannot turn to God.

Repentance: that's what is needed, if he is ever to be honest and decent in his philosophy ...

. . .

Side by side on his sofa.

WITTGENSTEIN: My heart is empty.

ME: Then let me fill it.

WITTGENSTEIN: The door of my heart is shut.

ME: Then let me open it.

His arm around my shoulders. His hand on my thigh. His face turned to mine. The *depths* from which his eyes look out.

WITTGENSTEIN: Do you know how beautiful *you* are? Do you know what you mean to me? You are close to God, you know. For me, you are close to God. (A pause.) God is not *for* the innocent. The innocent are *of* God. The innocent *are* God. (Whispering:) God is very close to us. He is here, in this room.

We lie together (that's what he calls it: *lying together*).

The early hours. He speaks of his confession.

Sincerity—that's what he dreams of. Honesty. But honesty so great that we speak of more than we know. A sincerity so great that we no longer *know* what we will say.

One day, we will live and breathe in truth, he says. And there will be no end to truth.

And God will live in our hearts, he says. And our love will be God's love.

And our love will be *of* God, *with* God.

16th December

His rooms.

I read him one of my poems. He makes a face.

WITTGENSTEIN: Yes, yes, it is very pretty. Very pastoral. You know the names of all the animals. But ours is not the time for poems of that kind.

I read him another poem, about love.

WITTGENSTEIN (shaking his head): Why do you think you have the *right* to write of such things?

Love is unutterable, he says.

Coldham's Common.

He speaks of the indecency of light. Of the white sky that sees nothing, but that sees nonetheless.

Blindness watches, he says. And there are no secrets left, nothing hidden.

It's as though light had permeated his body, he says. As though his innards were filled with light.

He speaks of white light, like a fog drifting through him. He speaks of the whiteness and opacity of the sky flowing through him.

He wants to hide, he says. He wants to cower.

He speaks of madness seething inside him. Rocking inside him. He speaks of madness coming to his edges.

WITTGENSTEIN: Do you know what an effort it is simply to keep my balance?

(A long pause.) Do you see what you've done to me, Peters? What you're *doing* to me?

(A long pause. Quoting:) *We have rolled on the floor of the squares of Babylon. Lust grows up like brambles above our heads.*

ME: We've done nothing to be ashamed of.

WITTGENSTEIN: Oh, there's nothing for *you* to be ashamed of. (Quoting:) *For the good man, there is not evil possible, whether it be living or dead.* (A long pause.) I do not deserve you.

ME: Of course you do!

WITTGENSTEIN: You mustn't grow old like me ... *It is forbidden to grow old ...*

ME: You're not so very old.

WITTGENSTEIN: But I am corrupt. I am ugly.

ME: You're none of those things.

17th December

Morning. I lie on his sofa as he works at his desk. Open notebooks. An open ledger. Facedown: a copy of Ignatius's *Spiritual Exercises*.

A look of absolute concentration on his face. Absolute intensity. Is this what thinking looks like? Is this what a *philosopher* looks like?

Wittgenstein leans back in his chair. Sighs.

WITTGENSTEIN: I give in! I can't work with you around!

I tell him that I'm being as quiet as I can. That I want nothing more than to watch him work.

He speaks of his hatred of self-consciousness. Of self-*awareness*. Absorption, that's his ideal. The mind must be absorbed in its activities.

But when the mind's problem *is* the mind?, he wonders. When the mind's problem is the very impossibility of absorption?

He sends me home so he can *get on with things*.

I text Ede: *Am W.'s boyfriend*. Ede texts back: *About time*.

I update my Facebook status: *In a relationship*. Mulberry writes on my wall: *No fucking way*. I write back: *Way*.

Five o'clock. No text from Wittgenstein. Six. Still no text. Seven. I text: *I'll bring you dinner*. Eight: still no reply.

18th December

No Wittgenstein. He's not in his rooms. He doesn't reply to texts.

I flick through the *Confessions* in the library.

19th December

Evening. Wittgenstein texts, very curt. *Back from London to-morrow. Meet me 11 AM—station.*

He was in London?

20th December

Cambridge Station. Wittgenstein, unsmiling. His flat cap. His rucksack. He looks worn.

I've been reading Augustine, I tell him.

Silence.

I've missed you, I tell him. Cambridge has been very dull.

Silence. The tension in his face increases.

I ask him what's the matter.

The train was full of dons, he says.

Dons in suits. Dons wired up, networked. Dons plugged

in, keeping in touch. Dons tapping away on iPads, consulting spreadsheets and flow diagrams. Counting their citations on Google Scholar. Watching for 'likes' on their Facebook posts. Dons on the phone *touching base … reaching out …*

Dons looking out with approval at the low-rise homes being built at Clay Farm. At the new office complexes being built round Addenbrooke's. At the new multistorey car parks. At the new biomedical campus.

Dons, with *Silicon Fen* on the brain. With the *Cambridge Cluster* on the brain. With the *Northwest Development* on the brain. With the *knowledge economy* on the brain.

How many days are left?, he says. How many days can there be? Surely this is the end. Surely things are coming to an end.

But that's just it: nothing is ending, he says. That's it: the eternity of the end. The endlessness of the end.

Hell—*this* is Hell. *Because* there are no flames. *Because* it does not burn him.

He cannot stay here, he says. Cambridge is destroying him.

He does not want it to end here—in Cambridge.

Anywhere but here, he whispers. Anywhere but here.

WITTGENSTEIN: God protect me. God help me.

Later, in his rooms.

He goes straight to work.

I fall asleep on the sofa. He lays a blanket over me.

21st December

Wittgenstein, vexed at what he called my *superficial conversation* with the porter in the lodge.

WITTGENSTEIN: You must be careful, Peters. You are corruptible. You have not fought for your innocence. That is clear.

ME: I was only joking with him!

WITTGENSTEIN: You are becoming thoughtless and stupid.

I tell him I'm sorry.

WITTGENSTEIN: But you have no understanding of what you should be sorry *for*.

Wittgenstein stops, and holds his left wrist in his right hand.

His heart beats too fast, he says.

I take his wrist in my hand.

He pulls it away.

He is becoming anxious—terribly anxious, he says.

WITTGENSTEIN: Perhaps it would be better if you and I didn't see one another.

My tears.

I remind him of what he said: that it was only by weeping that you can drive the splinter of philosophy from your heart.

WITTGENSTEIN: But the splinter of philosophy lies in *my* heart, not yours.

Town. We walk among the shoppers in the pre-Christmas sales.

He points out the street corner the street-cleaning machines always miss.

Litter. Torn things. Dirtied things. Bits of plastic and metal and paper. Rubbish slowly turning into pulp.

The world is mired in filth, he says. It is drowning in filth.

Even Cambridge, he says. *Especially* Cambridge.

He's becoming wicked, he says. He's treated me cruelly, he knows it.

He's reached a decision, he says. He plans to resign. To leave Cambridge.

I nod my head mutely.

WITTGENSTEIN: I'm sorry. I know you won't understand.

I tell him I *do* understand. That I understand *everything*. The dons … The university … They don't appreciate him.

WITTGENSTEIN: It is more than that.

I tell him that we students never took him seriously enough.

WITTGENSTEIN (quoting): *Above all else, guard your heart.*

ME: I thought you said I would save you. That I was close to God.

WITTGENSTEIN: *The closer one comes to God, the more one sees oneself as a sinner.* (A pause.) Do you know what sin is, Peters?

ME: I don't believe in sin.

WITTGENSTEIN: Then you understand nothing.

23rd December

The Palm House, at the Botanic Gardens. Orchids and passionflowers in the canopy above us.

He recounts a dream. Of the Arctic expanse. Of the aurora borealis flashing in the sky. Of a palace of ice, and of his brother in the great hall among narwhal horns and white furs and amber—his blue-lipped brother, playing with shards of ice, rearranging them, moving them around ...

In his dream, he has gone to rescue his brother. But his brother is lost in his ice puzzle, and does not know him. His brother does not even know his own past—the attic room; the house, with its piano and its basement study; the pathless woods outside ...

And then, in his dream, he is heading south. Over the tundra, over the snowfields and the sheet-ice. Through the frozen air.

The first trees—stunted larches. Then pine trees, a few at first. Then forest, dark with conifers.

Then the first road. The first hamlets. The first patches of brown earth.

South, towards home. South, his brother's step inside his own. His brother's life inside his own. South, to where the mountains rise and the valleys deepen. South, to their attic room in their childhood home.

• • •

The Oceanic Islands display. Lavender and giant daisies.

WITTGENSTEIN: I'm leaving tomorrow. In the morning.

ME (stupidly): But you'll have to pack.

WITTGENSTEIN: They will pack for me. They will send on my things.

ME: Where are you going?

He shakes his head.

ME: You're not even going to tell me where you're going?

He shakes his head again.

ME: Will you take me with you?

A final *no*.

I tell him I don't want to be alone in Cambridge. I tell him I'm afraid.

He tells me I should think about God very, very hard. He smiles.

ME: Will you come back for me?

I tell him I want to see him driving up to my rooms in a white limo with a bunch of roses, waving at me through the open sunroof. I tell him I want him to clamber up my fire escape and gather me up and kiss me. *What did the student do when his teacher came to rescue him?*, he'll say. *He rescued him right back*, I'll say.

Night. His rooms.

His mother used to lead a quintet who performed a Christmas concert every year in the Stadtcasino in Basel, he says. He and his brother used to love watching them play. Their give-and-take. Their musical *courtesy*. Their musical *friendship*.

There was a sense of *imminence* in their playing, he says.

Of *urgency*, quite detached from concerto-thrills. It was about the present. About the *moment*, thick with promise. You felt that the world was about to change completely …

It frightened him back then, he says: the thought that the world could change completely. But now?

After philosophy, the revelation will be continuous, he says. Theophany will be continuous. Every moment will be full to bursting.

After philosophy, every moment will be a Sabbath, and time will be a movement only from Sabbath to Sabbath.

After philosophy, we will know things as they are, he says. We will *be* as we are.

After philosophy, everything we say will be true.

Night. We lie together.
      We lie together.
      We lie together.

Late. Snow-light outside.
      Noise from the courtyard. Voices shouting.
      Is it Guthrie?, he says.
      Guthrie's gone home, I tell him.
      WITTGENSTEIN: You must go home. Tomorrow, when I leave, go home, Peters. Get the train north.
      We must all go home, he says. Everyone must go home …
      Philosophy is really homesickness, he quotes. *The desire to be at home everywhere.*

·   ·   ·

The early hours. He wakes up shaking.

WITTGENSTEIN: Oh God, it's here. Madness is here.

His fear that his mind will burst. His *hope* that his mind will burst.

To undo his mind. To *release* it.

What will he become, when he welcomes madness? When he *affirms* madness?

What will he become, when he falls into his madness? When madness *falls through him*?

He knows he is going mad, he says. He knows that these are the last days of his sanity.

He does not want to be alone at the end. He knows he will be alone at the end.

He's afraid of madness, he says. That madness it will leave something of him left.

He's afraid that madness *will not obliterate him*.

Dawn.

Still shaking.

His *confession*. He speaks of his life. Of what he has been. Of what he has *done*.

He speaks of his sins. Of the past. He speaks of all those who have been lost.

He says that he, too, will soon be lost.

WITTGENSTEIN: Remember me, Peters.

. . .

After philosophy, every moment of the past will be remembered, he says. Nothing will be lost.

After philosophy, the past will be reparable, he says. Reversible.

After philosophy, death will be transformed into life, he says. Sorrow will be transformed into joy.

After philosophy, the dead will awaken. The dead will be reborn. His brother, his mother, his father: they will be reborn.

After philosophy, we will weep without cease. We will laugh without cease.

After philosophy, the world will open as his homeland. As *our* homeland.

After philosophy, we will know what it means to live.

Christmas Eve

Morning.

He is pale. Worn.

So he is still sane, he says. Still alive.

We should pray together, he says. We should thank God on our knees. A pause. And then: no, it is not for me to pray.

My youth is already a prayer, for him. My beauty: prayer in the flesh.

Am I his friend?, he asks me. I nod. And he says: yes, I am his friend. God has given him a friend.

Tears spring to his eyes.

WITTGENSTEIN: Do you see? I nearly wept …

I tell him he must stay. That he can't think of going anywhere, in his condition.

He says he won't stay. That this can't be where it all ends. Not here. Not in Cambridge.

The last moments, as we wait for his taxi.

Last night, he dreamt he came back to Cambridge, he says. That he came back to rescue me, and to be rescued in turn.

I didn't recognise him when he returned, he says. He'd come back in a new guise. He was himself—but he wasn't himself.

And he didn't know *me*, not immediately.

In his dream, it took time for us to find our way back to one another. To court one another all over again, and in a new way.

In his dream, everything that has happened happened again, as if for the first time. Everything—his class, our walks on the Backs, our romance, even last night, even the night of sadness before his departure ...

In his dream, I found him again, he says. I saw him in someone else's face. He came towards me with every face but his own. He came *laughing*, he says. He came *weeping*. He came in *innocence*, as pure as a spring breeze.

The taxi draws up. The driver packs Wittgenstein's cases into the boot.

He will come back to Cambridge as a *judge*, he says. A sword will go out of his mouth to smite his enemies. And I will sit at his right-hand side, and Ede at his left.

The dons will bow their heads in repentance. The porters in their lodges will look up expectantly. The cleaners will pause with their vacuum cleaners and wait for a sign.

He will come back to Cambridge as a *lover*, he says. He will hold me in his arms. My hair will be thick against his mouth. My legs will be entwined with his. My fingers, wrapped round his fingers.

And he will sleep beside me, he says. I will sleep beside him. We will be gathered up in the hand of night. Held together.

He will come back to Cambridge as the *sanest man in the world*, he says. As a man who has passed through madness and survived. As a man remade in the crucible.

He will come as the *last thinker*, he says. As the *last philosopher*. He will wield germinal forces. *Cosmic* forces. He will burn with the great fire of God.

And the first morning of the world will dawn again, he says. The eternal New Year. And he will step with us all into the new world. The coming world.

And there will only be forces and densities, not forms and matters, he says. And there will be but currents and countercurrents, peaks and troughs, and nothing enduring.

And there will be nothing but God, he says. Nothing but divinity, angels torn apart. Nothing but the end, perpetually ending. Nothing but the beginning, eternally recurring.

After philosophy, we will have no names, he says.

After philosophy, there will be a name for everything, and not just for every *kind* of thing.

He embraces me. Presses a notebook into my hand.

It's all there, he says. His path into the pathless. The way out.

WITTGENSTEIN: Remember me, Peters.

He climbs into the taxi, his mackintosh folded over his arm. He's gone.